Book Three of the California Dreaming Series

For more information on my upcoming projects, please go to my website: www.rodneylamarr.com

Trigger Warning

This book contains sensitive material about death, trauma, suicide, sexual assault, and violence. If these topics are too much for you, for whatever reason, please do not continue reading this book. I appreciate you supporting my book, but your mental health is more important.

Dedication

This book is dedicated to you. Thank you!

Table of Contents

CHAPTER ONE 1

CHAPTER TWO 3

CHAPTER THREE 7

CHAPTER FOUR 11

CHAPTER FIVE 17

CHAPTER SIX 21

CHAPTER SEVEN 23

CHAPTER EIGHT 29

CHAPTER NINE 33

CHAPTER TEN...35

CHAPTER ELEVEN...39

CHAPTER TWELVE...43

CHAPTER THIRTEEN...49

CHAPTER FOURTEEN 53

CHAPTER FIFTEEN...57

CHAPTER SIXTEEN..59

CHAPTER SEVENTEEN..63

CHAPTER EIGHTEEN...65

CHAPTER NINETEEN 67

CHAPTER TWENTY 71

CHAPTER TWENTY-ONE...75

CHAPTER TWENTY-TWO...77

CHAPTER TWENTY-THREE...79

CHAPTER TWENTY-FOUR...81

CHAPTER TWENTY-FIVE..85

CHAPTER TWENTY-SIX...89

CHAPTER TWENTY-SEVEN...91

CHAPTER TWENTY-EIGHT 95

CHAPTER TWENTY-NINE 99

CHAPTER THIRTY..103

CHAPTER THIRTY-ONE...105

Chapter One

The Future

The storm clouds of death have hung over me for years, but I never knew just how much until today. I swallowed, watching the officer's ocean eyes drown with fear while the gun honed in on me. My breathing grew wild as my sister's screams echoed in the background, not finding their intended target.

His finger squeezed the trigger and a bright orange and white explosion erupted from the gun. A massive blast reverberated throughout the area, filling my ears with a piercing ringing sound.

As the bullets soared through the air, my soul embraced for impact. My body stiffened as the first explosion of pain hit. I gasped as the air escaped my lungs.

My life did not flash before my eyes, nor did a bright white flow over me. Instead, the reality of the moment held me down, ensuring I felt every moment of its existence.

Time slowed as I took in the scene. The officers stood frozen, leaning forward, bent knees, gripping their guns. Officer Wright's eyes were stuck, half closed and half opened.

His partner wore a more satisfying expression. His teeth dug into his bottom lip as his hand gripped the frozen gun, slightly angled from his firing position.

Their badges, wrapped with a black stripe, signified Death still loomed nearby. Its fingers tugged at their hearts as it set its eyes on me. I prayed it wouldn't come. Not here. Not now.

My heart sank when I turned to Miracle. Her tears appeared glued to her cheeks. The expression on her face reflected the pain my body now felt. Her brown eyes were an island around an ocean of white as her arms extended. Her mouth froze with the screams of a broken heart.

I turned back to find three bullets hanging perfectly in the air like stars on a moonlit night. Smoke traced their every movement while the sun glistened off their metal shells. And then…

Another heat-seeking explosion ripped my flesh, forcing me against the brick wall. Crimson snowflakes flurried on the dry cement.

My legs buckled underneath me, forcing my body to the ground. The cold cement blanketed my fall.

My body hurt. Every breath hurt. I slammed my eyes shut, trying to kick the pain away. But the pain was just too agonizing. Each impact forced the reality of the moment back into existence.

I didn't want to die. Not then. Not like that. I wanted to live. I wanted to LIVE!

Another scream cried out.

"WAITTTTTT!"

Chapter Two

The Present

"Yo, D up. D up."

"Watch the pick! Switch, switch."

I ran around Drake, rubbing against his shoulder as he stood posted at the three-point line. My defender bounced off Drake's body, leaving me wide open for the shot.

Marcus dribbled to his left and then crossed over to his right. When he saw me, he quickly hurled the ball in my direction. It landed securely in my hands and I turned my body and sprang up with one fluid motion. My arms extended as the ball quickly rolled off my fingertips.

While the ball soared to its final destination, my right arm froze in the air as one of my favorite sounds found its place in the world.

Swiiissssh.

"Nothing but net, baby," I shouted. I gave Drake a high-five and sprinted down the court. After a few more plays, our game ended like it usually did, with my team getting another W.

"Dre," a familiar voice shouted. I jogged over to find Miracle waiting on the sidelines.

"What up, sis?"

We exchanged our usual greetings, which ended in a hug.

"Eww, gross." Her fingers pinched her nose as she jerked backward. "What the hell?"

I raised my arm and took a sniff. It wasn't *that* bad.

"This is how real men smell. My bad." I shot her a smile, but it wasn't returned. I offered my towel, which she gladly accepted.

"Anyways, Autumn wants to know if she can interview you for a project she's working on."

"Big booty Autumn?" Another smile, but like before, it wasn't returned. "I'm kidding, sheesh. Sure, I'll do it," I said.

"Awesome."

"Wait, do I get paid?" I asked.

"Nope," she said.

"Then what's in it for me?"

"You'd be helping out your sweet lil' sister, big bro." Miracle's eyes widened as her bottom lip protruded out, clearly the worse puppy dog eyes I had ever seen.

"Are you constipated or something?" Her hand swung in my direction without warning, smacking against my arm.

"Dang, Floyd Mayweather. I'm just kidding, sheesh." I rubbed my arm, trying to figure out how this little girl could hit so hard. "This is why mom and dad like me more. You're too violent."

She raised her fist for another punch, but I lifted my hands in defense and stood on the balls of my feet. I wasn't about to let my little sister beat me up.

"I ain't scared of you," I paused, "anymore."

"Stupid." She rolled her eyes and finally allowed herself to smile.

"Okay, I'll do it. I'll hook up with Autumn after school."

"Bet. Thanks, Dre."

"Aight. I'm about to show these boys how to ball. I'll catch you later."

I hopped back on the court. After a few moments, I turned and saw Miracle walk into the quad. My smile slowly vanished as I stared off into the distance.

"Yo, Dre. You playing?" Drake asked.

I turned back, smiled and played one more game.

After the final basket, some of the guys and I walked off the court. We didn't have enough time to play another game, so we opted to get ready for class. Marcus and a few others stayed on the court and shot the ball around.

"Good game, bro."

"Thanks, Drake. You too," I said as sweat dripped down my face. If I didn't stink before, I certainly do now.

I flopped onto the bench and extended my legs to get a good stretch. My shoes came off with a few tugs as I let my feet breathe in the crisp autumn air.

My forearms pressed against my knees as my head hung down. I sat, watching leaves dance between my feet while my lungs burned from the treacherous pace on the court.

I usually didn't struggle this much, but lately, struggling to keep up with the guys had become the norm. Still, my team squeezed by with another nail-biting victory.

My hand slid into the front pocket of my backpack, looking for my towel when the red bracelet accidentally flopped onto the ground.

I scooped it up, brushing off the dirt. Thoughts of Ash quickly swam into my head, making everything else obsolete.

Chapter Three

The Past

"Ouch." My head jerked back as my hand flew to my neck.

Ash pulled away with an innocent smile on her face.

"Did you just bite me?"

"I always feel like biting you," Ash said.

"Yeah, that's weird."

She smiled. "I think it's a woman thing."

I frowned.

"My mom used to always bite my dad, too. She said it was because she loved him so much; she always had the urge to bite him."

"Maybe you and your mom are vampires or something, because that ain't normal." I double-checked one last time. *Still no blood.*

Ash pulled me into her, leaning her head on my chest. I flinched at first, but the fear gradually subsided and I embraced her too.

"What was your mom like? You never talk about her," I asked.

She paused for a second and then spoke.

"She was amazing. Fierce. Stubborn." She smiled as thoughts of her mom floated from Heaven. "We had so much fun together. She was real cool."

She paused for a moment, staring into the emptiness. I gave her time. My shoulders drooped down when thoughts of my mom crept into my head.

"After she died, my dad and I struggled to figure out how to survive." She bit her bottom lip and nodded. "I wasn't the most *supportive* child. We're cool now, I think. But he still worries. A lot."

A calm silence rested between us. I felt her heart beat against my chest. I squeezed her, letting her know I was there for her. Eventually, she spoke once again.

"I miss her."

She looked up into my eyes. There was sadness there, but she didn't cry. Her strength wouldn't allow her to cry, not in front of me. Once, she told me she would never cry in front of me because she was an "ugly crier," whatever that meant.

"Well, I got you." I pressed her into me. "Nothing will happen when I'm with you."

She patted me on my chest, "Okay, Superman."

I shrugged. "Superman? More like Black Panther, or what about Luke Cage?"

She smirked. "Have you seen your muscles?" she said sarcastically. Her hand curled into a ball, covering her laugh.

"Oh, you got jokes, huh?" I leaned back, turning my head to avoid eye contact.

"Ah, my baby upset," she said, mocking me in her best baby impression. "Momma's got *you*."

She slid her hands along my cheeks. The softness of her hands felt like sunshine. The sweetness of her perfume teased my senses. She leaned in, pressing her forehead against mine and whispered, "I got you."

Our lips met as her arms found a home around my shoulders. She leaned into me and I leaned into her.

Her loop earrings tapped the side of my neckline as she tilted her head close to mine. My hands roamed across her back, massaging the goosebumps that had just appeared.

Ash wasn't the first person I ever kissed. But she was the only person I would never forget.

She adjusted her body so her back was now leaning on my chest. I slung my arm around her and began twirling the red braided bracelet on her left wrist.

□■□■

"Dre. Earth to Dre!"

I shook my head and looked up. Drake was standing over me, already fully dressed. He wiped his towel across his head, leaving tiny white pieces of cloth resting in his hair.

"You good, my dude? You've been staring into space for a good ten minutes," he said.

"What? Yeah, I'm fine. That game wore me out, man," I said, extending my legs for another stretch. "I can't keep up with these young freshmen anymore."

"I feel that. Alright, bro, I'll catch you in class."

"Aight."

My fist collided with his as he turned to walk away. I glanced at the bracelet, sliding my fingers inside as it hugged my wrist. I allowed myself one last thought of Ash and wished her a sweet farewell.

Chapter Four

The Present

After school, I met up with Autumn and proceeded to her house. I had been to her home a few times to get Miracle, but this would be the first time I went inside the large brickstone house.

"Hey, guys," Autumn said.

"Hey, sweetie," her mom said from the living room. Multiple IDs jingled against her dark blue scrubs as she talked. Her short salt and pepper hair accentuated her narrow face.

"Hey, baby girl," her dad said. "And who is this?" he asked with raised eyebrows, not caring enough to stand up or lower his coffee mug.

"This is Andre," she said. "Miracle's brother. He's helping with my podcast."

"Hello, Sir. Ma'am." I waved. The mom greeted me with a half-smile and the dad just nodded.

"Hmm. Usually, parents love me," I thought.

Seemingly ignoring her parents, Autumn stepped into the kitchen while I stood in the entryway. I slid my hands into my pockets and rocked back and forth on my tippy toes.

Jars clang together as Autumn rummaged through the refrigerator. After a few minutes, her head peaked over the door.

"Want something to eat?"

"No, I'm fine, thanks," I replied.

Autumn grabbed an apple and then proceeded to the pantry. Her parents returned to their discussion about a patient having gastro something or other. I couldn't follow their conversation, so I turned my attention to the house.

A lavender aroma blanketed the space as multiple certificates lined the nearby oak bookshelf, filled with medical-related books. Black and white family pictures squeezed into rectangular frames and hung perfectly aligned on the walls. Most highlighted the growth of Autumn.

There was a picture of her parents staring at their chubby-cheeked baby wrapped in a fuzzy pink blanket. Another had a young Autumn smiling as a brown sash sprinkled with various patches slung over her shoulder.

"Never would have guessed she was a Girl Scout," I thought.

Next to it was an image of a teenage Autumn forcing a smile as she stood between her parents; a beautiful beach sunset hung in the background.

"Ready?"

Autumn's words broke my focus and I nodded. I followed her to a room in the back of the house. Black spiked cubes clung to the walls, providing a soundproof environment. A red microphone sat on a glass-top desk in the center of the room. Her laptop and camera were next to it.

"Okay, so you'll sit there and I'll be here," she motioned to two chairs.

"And what exactly are we doing?" I asked.

"I'm doing a series called 'The People' where I interview folks from our neighborhood."

There was an uncommon confidence in her voice as if she had been doing this her entire life. I wondered if her voice was what a teenage Michele Obama would sound like. Powerful yet hadn't fully reached her full strength.

I scrunched my face. "And you want to interview me?" My hand covered my mouth as the realization became clear.

"Yeah," she nodded. "People love you, Dre. You're popular." She raised a finger as if she was reading off a list. "You're funny." Another finger. "And...," she paused, seemingly hesitant. "You're fine as *hell.*" A giant smile crossed her face. Her smile looked like a girl who always got what she wanted.

"Oh," I said, not returning her smile. Instead, I avoided eye contact, focusing on a box of notebooks in the corner. The thought of being in the spotlight concerned me.

"Well?" She waited for my response. I guess my hesitation was interpreted as a yes, somehow. She quickly turned and began setting up her laptop.

A ring light switched on, emitting a sharp brightness that burnt my eyes. With a few hits to her keyboard, the light slowly dimmed to a tolerable level. Then our reflections appeared on the laptop screen.

"All you have to do is relax and answer some questions." She swiveled around in her chair. "Okay?"

"Sure, yeah," I stuttered.

I adjusted my body based on her directions and the interview began. She greeted her fans and welcomed them to the Autumn's World podcast. Then she introduced me. I smiled and waved, trying to hide my nervousness.

On the screen, I appeared confident, but inside, a wave of nausea swept through my body. My stomach felt empty like a vast desert and I could feel my pulse boom with every beat.

Her face went from the camera to me and the professional Autumn soon appeared.

"Dre, what are your plans for the future? What do you want to do after high school?"

"Well," I said, "honestly, I haven't really spent much time thinking about it." I licked my lips, trying to quelch the dryness. "I know college for sure, but I still haven't found my purpose after high school, ya know?"

She nodded and set her pecan brown eyes on mine; a sense of calm rushed over me. *"Dang, Autumn was good,"* I thought.

I continued. "Probably something with kids."

"Kids?" Autumn questioned.

"Yeah, I mean, recently, I've been thinking about becoming a teacher or coach or something."

"What made you have that thought?"

"Honestly?" I paused. A gentle smile crossed my lips as thoughts of Miracle flowed within me. "My little sister. My little sister is the most amazing person I've ever met and ya know, as her big brother, it's my job to look after her."

My hesitation disappeared and my mind and my mouth flowed with ease.

"But sometimes, I feel like she's *my* big sister. I try to teach her how dumb guys can be and to be street smart, but she teaches me how to be a better dude."

"Miracle's cool like that," Autumn added. "What exactly does she teach you?" She leaned forward, waiting for my response.

"How to love and how I deserve to be loved, ya know? Don't get me wrong; I'm no punk or anything. But she has a unique way of making people feel special, inspiring people to aim for greatness. That's what I want to give to others, especially kids."

I swallowed and then leaned forward.

"It's hard surviving in these streets."

Autumn smiled and nodded her head in agreement. She asked me a few more questions about my life and future plans. Then, she focused on more serious topics.

"With the craziness of what is happening in the nation these last few years and the stupidity of some folks in our school…." Autumn began. Her voice turned sharply at that last statement as if something was lying dormant in her mind. She continued, "do you think our local community has problems with racism?"

My lips parted, but nothing came out. I wasn't expecting such a profound question from a freshman in high school.

I leaned back in my chair as my mind swirled with thoughts of the past. Anger engulfed me as I clenched my jaw and my breathing quickened. I held my head down and tried to calm myself before I began to speak.

"We have a few," I paused and took in a shaky breath, "people with racist minds. Sadly, the few affect so many."

"Have you seen it in our school?" Autumn asked.

My answer was filled with anger and I needed no hesitation.

"Yes!"

Autumn ended the interview and thanked me for my time. I was amazed by her skill in front of the camera, even though I knew that wasn't where I belonged. I said my goodbyes to her and her parents and slowly walked home.

Chapter Five

The Present

The heavy wooden doors opened as a stream of light blinded me. My hands immediately shielded my eyes as a floral aroma lingered in the air while silence filled the room.

As my eyes slowly adjusted, white stoned walls held beautifully decorated stained-glass windows. One depicted a black man sprawling his arms, casting intolerance out and welcoming forgiveness, while a rainbow hung in the background, hugged by various shades of blue, like the ocean itself.

I stepped forward. The pews were void of life, yet a soft whimper of crying emerged from the silence. The crying grew louder. Then, the agonizing plea from a grieving mother shook me.

It was my mother, my mom.

I looked up. There she was, dressed as the night itself. Her hands covered her face as tears seeped through her fingers. The low, growling sound of heartbreak escaped her lips as she dropped to one knee.

Not far away, my dad stood like a statue-version of himself, staring into the abyss. His face was emotionless. His sunken eyes were void of life.

My sister was a shadow of my mom. Her arms wrapped her soul as tears pooled at her feet.

"Hello?" I shouted, but there was no reaction.

"Mom? Dad?" Still no response. I stepped forward, closer to my grieving family.

As I approached, the faint sound of a heartbeat emerged from the depths of my soul. With every step, it grew louder until its existence brought pain to mine.

"Mom," I shouted…still nothing.

I stood a few feet away as a long coffin appeared beside her. The silver glistened off the dim-lit chandelier that hung from the ceiling. My mom's hand pressed against it.

I stepped closer, peering inside to see the cause of such grief. When I placed my hand on the coffin, a shock rippled through my arm, landing on my inner being.

"Dang," I mumbled.

Suddenly, the crying stopped. I turned back to my mom, who had vanished, as did my dad and sister. The church was no more; only death-like darkness floated around me. The only entities that remained were me and the unknown corpse inside.

I leaned over the coffin again as the body slowly became visible. First, a shoulder and an arm, dressed in a dark black suit. A red tie kissed the body's neck as my eyes scanned higher.

I let out an audible gasp as my eyes set upon a young man. There was nothing remarkable about him, minus the two-inch scar on his chin that never fully healed after being tossed from his bike when he was seven. His chubby cheeks and nose reminded people of his dad, "a spitting image," most would say.

I stood, jaw lowered, staring at my own reflection.

Bump bump!

More heartbeats. This time louder, stronger, more intense.

Bump bump!

I cringed at the sound, slamming my eyes shut, hoping that would relieve some of the pain.

Bump bump!

When my eyes opened, my lips…I mean, my reflection's lips were moving. Mumbling something, but it was too soft to hear.

I leaned closer. The smell of death hit me, causing me to jolt backward. His words were louder but still too faint to comprehend.

Bump bump!

My head was now inches away. My eyes trained on his lips.

"What?" I shouted back. "I can't hear you."

Suddenly, his eyes shot open, revealing haunting black eyes peering into the windows of my soul. His arm reached out as his boney fingers wrapped around my neck.

I grasped his wrist and arched back. But his strength was too much. He began pulling me into him, into the coffin.

"Get off me," I mumbled.

My airway constricted as his fingers squeezed harder, tighter. The world began to go dark.

"DIE!" it shrieked. The voice was not of this world.

With my final breath, I mumbled, "Get the hell…" Before I could finish, he dragged me into the coffin and the lid shut. Darkness.

I shot up, finding myself in the stillness of my bedroom.

Sweat trickled down my face, merging with my already-soaked t-shirt. The sound of raindrops tap dancing on the window echoed as thunder boomed in the background. Mirrored reflections of the lightning branches streaked across the room.

I lay back down. The street lights beamed through the window blinds, causing perfectly uniform beads to reflect on the ceiling. Then, I turned to my right to find the neon glow of my alarm clock. 2:45.

Chapter Six

The Present

Around 6:27, I dragged myself into the shower. It felt refreshing as the cold water splashed against my face, partially waking me from my comatose state.

After the shower, I slipped on a pair of basketball shorts, then my blue jeans on top. My throwback blue Kobe jersey came next, followed by the matching Los Angeles ball cap. I slid the final item onto my wrist; the red fabric bracelet. I stared at the bracelet and smiled.

Nowadays, this bracelet and my memories were my only genuine smiles. All the other ones were masks I wore to conceal my actual thoughts.

The clock read 6:58. There was still time. I moved to the nightstand next to my bed, pulled out a piece of paper and pencil and began writing.

□■□■

Love Letter # 363

'Dear Ash,

My grandma, Madea, used to pray each night and when I was younger, I thought it was silly. You see, every night, she would pray to see the sun one more time. As a kid, it didn't make sense to me, but now, I get it. Because you are my sun and ever since you left me, I have been praying every night to see you again. You were why I would wake up each day and your shine let me see true beauty for once in my life. I miss the sun. I miss my sun. I miss you so much that it hurts.

I paused. I needed a moment for my body to stop shaking before I could continue.

Do you know what I miss the most about you? I miss the sweetness of your voice and how when you spoke, birds would stop chirping to hear your sweet melody.

I know you will probably not come back to me. Some things just can't be taken away and I truly am sorry for not being what you needed. I do hope that one day; I can see your shine again!

"*Another letter that will probably go unread,*" I thought. But I didn't care. I wanted Ash to know how I felt. She had to know I still wanted her back; this was the only way I knew how to do it. I placed the letter in an envelope, sealed it and placed a stamp in the corner. I slid the envelope into my backpack and promised to mail it later that day.

Chapter Seven

The Present

In the afternoon, Miracle and I walked into the convenience store and flashed the clerk a quick nod.

"What's up, Dre," Kumar, the cashier, said as Miracle and I stepped past an old lady buying scratch-off lottery tickets.

"What's up, bro," I said. I shot him a nod and followed Miracle to my favorite part of the store.

"Red?" I asked while placing the plastic cup under the spout. I didn't need an answer. We always got a red Slurpee. Most of the time I had forgotten they even had more options.

I slid the straw into the wide cup opening while my sister poured a heaping pile of cheese over the container of chips.

Ding Ding

The front door chimed, capturing my attention and taking me back to her.

□■□■

Ash walked inside and I followed. The chime announced our arrival as we stepped into the convenience store. Ash walked over to the store attendant, gave him a fist bump and continued down the aisle. I didn't know him, so I settled for a quick nod and he did the same.

"Man, I used to eat these as a lil' kid," I said, pointing to a pack of strawberry Zingers.

"Gross, you need some real food like this." She pointed to a pack of miniature muffins. "Or maybe some of these." This time she pointed to a pack of gummy bears. "I'd tear you little bears up," she said, talking directly to the little bag.

"Do you want me to leave you two alone or something? Because this is getting a little weird," I asked, raising one eyebrow.

"Stupid," she said, swatting my arm.

"I'm just saying. I was getting a little jealous."

She rolled her eyes and kept walking.

"Got it." She walked up to the counter, where three tubs of frozen juices swirled.

"A Slurpee?" I scrunched up my face.

"Yeah, a Slurpee," she said, mocking me.

"Nah, I'm good. I'm not five years old." I turned to walk away.

"Oh my God," she said, practically screaming. I turned back around.

"What?"

"You've *never* had a Slurpee before, have you?" Her eyes widened and her mouth slowly fell open. She waited for my response.

"Uh…maybe when I was a kid, I don't know. I don't remember," I shrugged.

Her hand clenched onto mine, jerking me forward.

"I'm about to blow your mind." Her eyes were wide again and a gigantic smile crossed her face. Small dimples appeared that only revealed themselves when she smiled, like really smiled.

"What flavor do you want?"

I shrugged, but she ignored me. Ash looked like the black Vanna White as her hand glided between the three options. She waited for my response. Eventually, I gave in.

"Alright, girl. Sheesh. Uh, green apple."

She studied my face for a second and then picked up a large plastic cup. Ash grabbed the knob, pulled and a heap of red frozen lava poured out.

"Hey, I said green apple," I protested.

She didn't turn her head.

"No one gets green apple. You want red."

"Red? You mean cherry?"

This time she turned her head, revealing her scrunched-up face.

"We say red 'round here," she muttered with a southern drawl. It was so matter-of-fact that I had no other option but to nod.

"Red," I mumbled.

I turned away but quickly paused when I realized she wasn't behind me. When I looked back, Ash was busy piling a heap of flaming hot cheese over a container of chips. She turned to look at me, giving me her angelic smile. I just nodded.

After checking out, Ash and I sat on the curb. Her eyes went wild with excitement as she handed me the cup. She leaned in, watching my lips wrap around the straw.

I slurped up the icy goodness and my eyes sprung open. A cool sensation froze my inner self while the cherry taste embraced my taste buds, leading them in an elaborate synchronized dance of deliciousness.

Noticing my reaction, she began bobbing her head as a huge smile crossed her face. She gave me a playful nudge with her elbow, causing me to jerk to the side.

"Mmhmm. I told you," she said.

"Okay, you were right. This *is* good." I bowed slightly in her honor as she bounced her shoulders in a celebratory dance. I couldn't help but stare. She was gorgeous.

"Now, the nachos," she said, handing over the container.

"Ash, I've had nachos before."

"You've had movie theatre nachos and making-a-snack-at-home nachos, but you've never had gas station nachos." She nudged me with her shoulder again.

"Girl, you are crazy. And gas station nachos?" The thought was bizarre. "Are they better than my mom's nachos?" I reached for my phone.

Beep

Her eyebrows rose as she sat there momentarily; mouth open.

"I never said they were better than your mom's." She looked into the phone, "I would never say that, Mrs. Jenkins. I'm sure your nachos are the best!"

Her eyes moved to me and a frown crossed her face. I put the phone down.

Whack!

"You trying to get me in trouble with your mom?"

I leaned back as the laughter was uncontrollable.

"Nah, nothing like that," I chuckled. "We need moms to like you."

My eyes went to her and she looked back at me. Without saying another word, I reached into the container, grabbed a cheese-covered chip and slowly raised it to my mouth.

Her mouth opened as if she was about to take a bite too. Her tongue pressed against her top lip and I couldn't help but stare.

"Well?" she said, waiting for me to take the plunge. My eyes shot up to hers, momentarily embarrassed.

"Huh?" I shook my head. "Oh yeah."

The chip crunched in my mouth as the cheese splashed against my taste buds. Dang, it. She was right again. I reached for another chip and then another.

With a mouth full of chips, I looked her in the eyes and mumbled, "so good."

She smiled and said, "The food of the Gods."

I smiled. "Right!"

She lifted a chip and we cheered, "The food of the Gods."

After we devoured the chips we started our walk to her house. My fingers intertwined with Ash's as our feet moved in sync down Sierra Highway. We shared laughs like school kids and created imaginary worlds of the future. Our trip to her neighborhood only took ten minutes, but we managed to stretch it to thirty.

"Look," she said, pointing at the steel parallel lines at our feet.

"The old train line?"

"Dre, one day, I will get out of here and explore the world. I want to go to Maryland and see the Martin Luther King memorial or the Nelson Mandela Capture Site in South Africa; to New Zealand, too; maybe Atlanta."

"Atlanta?" I asked.

"Okay, that one is just for the lemon pepper wings. But the others are for educational purposes." She stuck up a finger for emphasis. "Don't you want to go anywhere?"

I paused and stared at the tracks. "Guess I never thought about it. Didn't think it was an option."

She turned my body to face hers and set her eyes on mine.

"Well, now it is. Anywhere. You can go anywhere. Where would it be?"

I thought for a moment. My smile slowly faded as I stared at her. I have studied every inch of her face before, but I still got lost in her beauty.

The sun hit her smooth caramel cheeks perfectly, revealing small dimples.

"Can I just go with you?"

She looked into my eyes. "You want to come with me?" she asked.

I stepped closer and grabbed her other hand. I tucked a single strand of her braid and carefully placed it behind her right ear.

She smiled, but I could tell she was waiting for my answer.

"I love you," I said. I didn't mean to say it. I meant to say yes, but my heart overpowered my mouth.

She looked down at the track while a gentle smile spread across her face. Her usually brown cheeks had a faint rosy glow to them. She looked back at me and leaned forward. Our lips nearly touched as she whispered, "I love you, too."

We kissed as she sank into my arms. Our bodies became one as we stood in the middle of the field, embracing like two people in love.

Our kiss lasted for what seemed like hours, but eventually, we had to get her home. When we approached her apartment complex, I stopped her.

"Are there black people in New Zealand?" I asked.

She thought for a second. "Only one way to find out."

□■□■

I blinked and I was back in the present. The memory of her brought a smile to my face and warmth to my heart.

"You, okay?" Miracle asked.

The moisture from the cup dripped on my hand as my sister stood there staring, scrunched face and all.

I smiled as my thoughts of Ash floated into the clouds.

"The food of the Gods," I mumbled. "Yeah, let's go."

Chapter Eight

The Present

When Miracle and I reached Rieko's apartment complex, I walked her to the community pool, where her best friend, Kim, was waiting, reading a book, as per usual.

Miracle and Kim were attached at the hip. She was practically my half-sister. I felt like she was at our house so much that she might as well move in. If she wasn't hanging at our house, Miracle was definitely at hers. But Kim was cool.

"Dang, does she ever *not* study?" I asked.

"Nah, that's her thing."

Kim peeked her head over the book. Her blue eyes shined as her braces sparkled in the sunlight, enhancing her expression. My two sisters embraced as if they hadn't seen each other in weeks.

"Aight, I'm going to find Rieko."

I shot them a wave and headed around the corner. Shortly after the pool disappeared, my heart sank and rage engulfed me. Erik Oliver and his stupid minion, Jake, stood roughly 20 yards away from me.

His buddy must have noticed me first because he nudged Erik and they both looked my way. Erik turned his slim frame towards me. The scars on his face first caught my attention, but his cold eyes stuck out to me.

My mom once told me that if you ever want to know the truth about someone, look into their eyes. Well, Erik's eyes were pure evil, no question about it.

A snarling dog slobbered at Jake's side as they approached. The beast was muscular and looked like a mix between a Pitbull, Doberman and a demon dog from hell.

"I know you," Erik said, pointing his finger in my face.

"Yeah, I know you too." I clenched my jaw as my eyebrows lowered. I could feel the veins in my neck pulsating.

"You're friends with, oh, what's her name?" Erik snapped his fingers while turning to his friend. Jake shrugged, gripping the metal chain constraining his monster of a dog.

"That's right. Ashley," Erik finished.

I lunged forward as his friend loosened the chain, sending the dog jumping in my direction. It was enough to stop my advance.

"You son of a ….," I yelled.

"How is Ashley anyways?" A mischievous smile formed on his lips as his eyes cast a death-like stare.

"Don't you ever say her name again! Do you hear me!"

I wanted to press forward, but his dog kept me at bay. I clenched my fists as my mind roamed for ways to get closer to him.

Suddenly, Miracle and Kim ran around the corner, stopping a foot behind me. I didn't want to involve my sister in this…neither of them.

"Look like you're playing for the wrong team, missy." I turned back to see Jake stretching his sausage-like finger in Kim's direction.

"Maybe she just likes dark meat," Erik said.

Kim folded her arms, sighing at the comment. Her eyes narrowed at Jake and then quickly flashed to the dog. There was a slight tremor in her body; she was no doubt scared of what the animal might do.

Suddenly, Jake's hand loosened, sending the dog lunging forward. Kim jumped back as her face went ghostly white.

The dog lurched forward, digging its nails into the ground, stretching its body towards Kim. I took a step between the two, but when it was mere feet away, Jake yanked the chain back, causing the dog to whimper in pain. Thankfully, it returned to Jake's side, but the threat was still present.

I quickly glanced at Kim to make sure she was okay. Her eyes were still honed on the dog. She was safe for now, so I turned back to Erik.

I felt steam roll off my head; all I saw was red. My mind circled with thoughts of Ash, thoughts that would drive any man crazy, but I had to focus on the task at hand.

I lowered my chin and raised curled fists in the air. I adjusted my positioning, making a smaller target for my opponent. No matter what, I refused to make this easy for them.

Jake followed my lead and prepared himself for a fight as well. Luckily, having to hold the chain caused him to be off-balance, a weakness I would remember to take advantage of if needed.

Unlike Jake, Erik didn't change his body positioning at all. He just lowered his head and stepped forward. I had to admit, that caught me off guard. He wasn't even defending himself. I stepped back, then forward, narrowing the distance between us.

He stepped forward again and I matched him. We were now maybe six feet away from each other. The dog lurched, digging his paws into the ground and pulling Jake forward.

As the fight was moments away, heavy footsteps pounded against the pavement, etching closer and closer. Rieko's broad-shouldered frame came into view as he raced by my side. His blue bandana bounced with every step.

I nodded and he returned the nod, trying to catch his breath. I noticed something in his right hand, but my angle didn't allow me to see exactly what it was.

Suddenly a streak of light reflected on Erik's face, causing him to squint from the brightness. The weapon must have been impressive enough for Erik to stop slithering forward. Instead, he and Jake held their positions as Rieko and I did the same.

I tilted my head forward to see Rieko's new weapon:

A machete.

Chapter Nine

The Present

My heart pounded with every second that went by. A grim smile emerged on Erik's face as my nerves went crazy, waiting for the fight to begin.

Thoughts of Ash floated into and out of my brain, causing the anger to build up repeatedly.

"I should have been there," I thought. I took a breath and reminded myself that it was not the time for those thoughts.

Finally, Erik turned, gave Jake a nod and quickly turned back to face me. I side-eyed Rieko and he nodded. This was it. That must have been their sign to throw the first punch. I clenched my right hand even tighter.

Left jab, right hook, I repeated in my head.

Left jab, then right hook.

"This has been fun," Erik said. Every word he uttered pissed me off even more. "We'll see each other real soon, my friend."

I didn't budge. I didn't trust him to walk away without trying some cheap shot. Jake pulled the dog's chain tighter, wrapping it around his wrist several times.

When Erik turned to walk away, his eyes made their way to Miracle. I could see fear in her eyes. She was strong, but the evil inside Erik could shake any mountain.

His finger pointed in her direction as that stupid smile emerged once again.

"Miracle, right?"

Heat erupted from within me and the anger overflowed.

"Don't talk to her! Don't you ever talk to my sister, you hear me?"

"Your sister, huh? Interesting."

I lunged forward, extending my arm towards his shiny bald head. But before I could make contact, I felt the heaviness of Rieko's stretched arm blocking my advance. I grunted as I thrashed in Rieko's grip.

Erik strolled away, disappearing around the corner. I struggled to move my gigantic friend out of the way. He was too strong and felt like a solid brick wall.

Eventually, I twisted my body free, or Rieko let me go. Either way I was fuming. I stomped back and forth, outraged by Erik's arrogance. My chest heaved up and down as my breathing grew erratic. I wanted to punch something…anything.

"Hey, Rieko?" a familiar voice sprouted out, interrupting my manic state.

"What's up, Miracle?"

"Where the hell did you get a machete?"

I paused and looked down at Rieko's right hand. I noticed Kim did the same. Finally, Rieko took a second to look at each one of our curious faces. He didn't respond. He just shrugged.

Miracle, Kim and Rieko shared a laugh, easing the tense moment. I looked at them and joined in, even though laughing was the last thing on my mind.

Chapter Ten

The Present

"How does that dude know you," I asked. Miracle shot Kim a glance before answering.

"He tried to start something yesterday at school," she said.

"What? Why didn't you tell me?" I asked.

"Figured it was over," Miracle said.

"Yeah, I totally forgot he lived in the neighborhood," Kim added.

"Yeah, I've seen him around here before. What beef he got with you two? Thought everyone loved you guys," Rieko said.

"He's a racist idiot. He has beef with most people, pure anger," Kim said. She nodded her head, showing her dissatisfaction with Erik's life choice.

"And you?" Miracle turned to me. "What was that all about?"

All eyes turned to me. My head turned away as I stared at a group of blue daisies. A bee sat perched on top of one. His world seemed far more uncomplicated than mine.

"Like you said, he has beef with everyone," I said.

Miracle studied me for a second as Kim and Rieko began walking away. She probably knew I was lying, but she didn't push it. For that, I was grateful.

I told Miracle I'd catch up with her later, so she headed back to Kim's apartment. I'd hoped they didn't run into Erik on the way back.

Moments later, Rieko and I stepped inside the small two-bedroom apartment he shared with his mom. His bedroom was covered with posters of celebrities dressed provocatively.

Beyonce was posed with her hand pressed against the side of her head; the yellow bikini provided a tremendous visual distraction. Then there was a black and white poster of Rihanna, causing my eyes to go straight to her thighs. Oddly enough, the last poster was of Betty White with the caption "Stay Golden."

I once asked him about that poster and his only response was, "What? Bro, B. White is a straight gangsta." I just nodded, afraid of what he might do if I disrespected "B. White."

"Have a seat. I'll put on the track." His voice trailed off as he sat in front of his laptop, searching for an audio file. After a few clicks, the song began. A low tribal beat slowly rose from the silence until a sweet drum mix joined in.

My head instantly began bobbing to the beat. He did the same. I closed my eyes and then was carried away by the moment. The beat had the precision of DJ Jazzy Jeff with the creativity of Kanye.

"That's clean, bro," I said.

"Right?" Rieko slowly raised his index finger as if he was on a rollercoaster, nearing the top. He flipped his finger down once another beat roared from the speakers. The mix was perfect. Before we knew it, our bodies swayed back and forth, letting the music take hold. For that brief moment, Erik didn't exist. My pain and heartbreak were distant memories. This is what I needed.

Rieko replayed the song a few times, sometimes even trying his hand at free-styling over the beat. I provided a few vocals, but neither of us could actually rap. Once the apartment concert was over, Rieko and I exchanged a few fist bumps and I relaxed on his bed while he looked for more beats.

"This music thing is you, man. You got Kanye talent, bro."

"My dude, I appreciate that, Playboy." He didn't turn around, but I knew he was smiling. He definitely had skills.

"So, what's up with that wonder bread?" he asked.

"Wonder bread? Oh, that dude. I think he or his brother did something to Ash." I held my head down and stared at my shoes.

"Word? That's why you were about to throw those hands?" He raised his fist in the air and began shadow-boxing, bobbing his head and rolling his shoulders like a professional fighter.

I didn't respond. He looked back at me and lowered his hands.

"Sorry 'bout your girl, Playboy. I liked her. I mean, she was cool. She looked good on your arm."

"Yep," I said, still not looking up.

"But you know Wonder Bread won't let this go, right? You know he'll be aiming for ya neck, right?"

I nodded. "Yeah, I don't think I can let this one go either. Not if he hurt Ash. I mean…" My voice trailed off, not sure how to express my thoughts.

Rieko nodded. "Yeah, I feel ya. You *need* something?"

I popped my head up, "Need something?"

"Come on, man. You know what I mean. Do you *need* to hold something?" He raised his hand and replicated a gun, pulling his finger back as if it were a trigger.

"Nah, I'm good."

"Bro…"

"I got something already," I mumbled.

"Word? Where did you get something from?" he asked.

My eyes fell to the floor and I didn't respond and he didn't push.

"Dang. Playboy is strapped up." He turned back to face his laptop. "Playboy is strapped up," he repeated.

Suddenly, all the memories of Ash and Erik came rushing back and so did the anger.

Chapter Eleven

The Present

My foot stepped against the solid white floor. I looked down and my reflection shined from the tiles below. My head flipped left then right, scanning my surroundings. There was nothing here. The smell of emptiness lingered in the air.

I walked forward, still looking around.

"Hello?" My voice echoed into nothingness.

As I moved forward, a set of stairs slowly came into view. I leaned over, trying to see where they led, but it was too far down.

I took in the scene around me, ensuring I didn't miss anything. Nope, still nothing but a white-colored void.

I swallowed and began descending. The stairs seemed to go down for hours. Step after step, never finding the bottom.

After what seemed like days, the bottom finally appeared; similar to the last area, it was as white as Christmas snow.

"Hello?"

Still no response. I slowly crept forward as an object appeared on the horizon.

I felt my steps turn into a full-out sprint. The object came closer until I realized it wasn't an object. It was a person. And it wasn't just *any* person…it was Ashley.

"Ash?"

I slowed my pace down until my sprint transformed into a brisk walk. My chest heaved up and down as I tried to catch my breath.

"Hey, Ash. What's going on?"

She didn't respond. Her back was to me. Her long white dress flowed in an imaginary wind. Her braids were tied together by a golden star, which hung against the middle of her back. Her head was slumped down.

"Ash, can you hear me?"

I stepped closer. The hairs on my skin stood up as I reached out. My hand found her shoulder and I twisted her body to face me. Her eyes stared into mine, but they were different. Her eyes had no light; the hope inside them was dead.

"Ash, what's going on?"

I leaned closer to her, but she just stared.

I called out to her again. Suddenly, she stepped back. And then again. She began taking slow, deliberate steps backward, increasing the distance between us.

"What are you doing? Where are you going?" I asked, stepping closer to her. But with every step I took, the further she seemed to get.

"Ash?" I screamed. My voice echoed in the emptiness.

She stepped back again and I stepped forward. I reached out for her hand, but she was too far away. Then, she suddenly stopped. A sinister smile spread across her face as she tilted her head. I screwed my face as I stared into her eyes.

"Ash?" My voice had lost all confidence.

And then, her arm extended forward, but her hand wasn't empty.

My hands shot up in defense as I screamed, "Ash!"

Her finger squeezed before I could say anything else and the blast erupted from the gun as a burning sensation tore through my chest.

My hands collapsed on my chest as blood pooled out. I fell to my knees and was then hit by another blast, sending me slamming against the now crimson-colored tiles.

Ash quickly divided the distance between us and before I could take another breath, she was leaning over me. Her eyes were of death and the same grim smile was painted on her face.

"Andre." A soft voice emerged from her lips. The gun barrel grew wide and her lips parted once again.

"Andre."

Her eyes were ice. Her finger yanked back on the trigger and…

"Andre!"

My head jolted up as my eyes popped open. The entire class stared at me, laughing as Mr. Haywood stood over me.

"Maybe if you stayed awake in my class, you would have done better on the quiz," he said, sliding last week's quiz onto my desk. My grade was written in giant red lettering; D-.

Mr. Haywood leaned down, placing his hand on my shoulder. "You used to be my best student," he whispered. "Anything I should know?"

I shook my head, examining the paper.

"No, I'll try harder, Mr. H."

He patted me on the back and continued to his desk.

The nightmares were getting worse. Everything in my life seemed to be getting worse. My mind was wrapped up in the past that I could never change. I needed to get over it. I needed to get over her. Unfortunately, when the bell rang, my mind returned to her once again.

Chapter Twelve

The Past

The sun glared in the sky as I sat outside on the wooden table in the school courtyard. Ash was sitting on top of the table, reading her newest book, *I'm Rising*. Rieko sat across from us, scrolling through his social media feeds.

I pressed play on my phone and the song instantly blared through the speakers. All three bodies swayed to the rhythmic sounds of Rieko's creation.

"This is fire, bro," I said as Rieko sat in anticipation. Ash closed her eyes, waving her hands in the air, while her book found a home on her lap.

"Thanks, Playboy. I hope to send off a few tracks to some folks this weekend." He glared back down at his phone, scrolling through some TikTok videos.

"Like, you're legit? You're about to make beats for a living?" Ash's eyes popped opened, intrigued by the thought.

"No cap, yo. I'm 'bout to do this music thang."

Ash shook her head.

"That's cool," she said.

"I can see someone like Joyner Lucas or maybe Kendrick Lamar doing a track on this one. This is fire," I repeated.

As the song ended, I extended my hand as Rieko did the same; our fists collided.

"My dude," he said. A giant smile crossed his face. He was proud of his talents.

"Y'all see they making a movie about that Riffenhowser dude? That joint crazy," Rieko said, pushing his phone in our direction.

"I feared for my life," Rieko mocked. "Let that have been a black guy; he'd be dead now. No cap."

"His name was Coffee," Ash said, looking up from her book.

"Whose name was Coffee," I asked.

"If Rittenhouse were a black man, his name would be Coffee," she said. Rieko looked at me. I shrugged.

Suddenly, one of Rieko's friends approached him and whispered something in his ear. A frown replaced his smile and he extended his hand once more.

"Aight, I gotta go handle some thangs. I'll holla, Playboy," he said. He looked at Ash and nodded, "Mrs. Playboy."

I gave him a pound and nodded.

Ash adjusted her body, pushing her legs under the seat, now sitting shoulder to shoulder with me.

"He has skills, Dre."

"I know, right? He's good."

"How did you guys ever hook up? I mean, you're complete opposites?" she asked.

I shrugged. "What do you mean?"

"You're sweet, Dre. Kind. You open doors for me, wrap your arms around me in public like you're not ashamed to be with me and let your boys see that."

"I mean, you are fine, so that helps," I joked. She shoulder-bumped me.

"I'm serious. That's rare for the other morons our age."

I smiled as a flush fell upon my cheeks.

"But Rieko," she paused. You could tell she was trying to choose her words carefully. "I'm just going to say it. He's a thug. I mean, look."

She motioned to the group of friends around Rieko. Blue shaded their clothes, as black-inked skin decorated their arms and necks. For some, tiny teardrops adorned the faces, revealing the harsh reality of the streets.

I glanced over; then, I looked back.

"Yeah, maybe. Rieko's a good dude. I've known him since we were kids."

"I'm pretty sure you and I went to the same school for a while, so that's not it," she said.

"He was with us in third grade. He…"

"Wait. You remember me from *third grade*?" she asked.

"Oh my God, girl. This isn't about you right now." I shot her a smile but kept going. "Rieko was in our class too, before he went to juvie." I paused so the information could sink in. "I met him before all that stuff. Before, he looked like the black Incredible Hulk."

She smiled.

"A few kids were picking on him and I stepped in and helped him out. We've been close ever since." I said it so matter-of-factly like it was supposed to happen like that.

"So how did he turn out...," she glanced again at Rieko, "like that and you turned out like, well you?"

"His whole family has been banging for as long as I could remember. He didn't have a choice."

I turned to look into her eyes. I was grateful she didn't give me the usual "everyone has a choice" speech. She grew up here, too and knew that sometimes options don't exist.

"Guess we don't all get the same choices in life." She stared off into the distance.

I stared off too.

"Guess not."

"What's up, guys?" A familiar voice broke our concentration.

We both turned to see my sister and Kim. Ash extended her hand and began a synchronized greeting involving a few high fives, fist bumps and booty bumps. Then, she did the same with Kim.

"Wait, what the hell," I said, shocked they already had a choreographed greeting.

The three ladies looked at me as if I was the crazy one. Ash retook her seat next to me as Miracle and Kim stood over us.

"What are y'all getting into?"

"Nothing, doing some people watching, as usual," Kim said, shining her bright smile in our direction.

"Anyone good?" Ash asked.

"Just you guys," Miracle said. "Actually, you guys squeeze together." Miracle commanded as she tilted her phone to the side, capturing a photo of Ash pressed against me as my arm wrapped around her body, our hands interlocked.

"Alright, we'll catch you guys later," Kim said, pulling her best friend away.

"See ya, bro. Bye, Ash," Miracle said.

"Deuces, guys," I said, throwing two fingers in the air.

"Your sister is cool. I like her," Ash said.

"Yeah, she's cool. I guess I'll keep her."

"You know I only hang out with you to get closer to her, right?" Ash leaned in, her glowing smile outshining the brightest stars.

"Oh yeah?" I asked, leaning my head toward hers.

Our lips were mere inches away as she whispered, "Yeah." My eyes went from hers to her lips and back to her maple-brown eyes. She smiled and then…

Our lips met and the rest of the world floated into the abyss. I slid my hand over her cheek as I went to hold her. She pressed her body against mine and our hearts synced up. Then she pushed me away excitedly.

"That's what I meant to ask you. Are you going to Tonya's party this weekend? Supposed to be a DJ and everything," she asked.

"I can't. My dad's forcing us to go to some barbeque with a few of his old Air Force buddies. They say, 'back when I was in,' and 'these young cats don't know how good they have it.'" I'm like, okay, we get it; you're old."

Ash stared at me as my rambling came to an end.

"I'm mean, I can't," I finished.

Her shoulders slumped as her smile vanished.

"It's cool." She grabbed her phone and mumbled loudly, "now, where did I put my side piece…oh here he is."

"Jokes." I waved my hand in the air pointing in her direction. "This girl right here has jokes."

She smiled and kissed my cheek. "Fine, I'll go with the girls or something."

"What girls?"

"You realize I have other friends when I'm not with you, right?"

"Word?" I joked, raising my eyebrows.

"Yeah, my world doesn't revolve around you, big head." She gently tapped two fingers on the side of my head.

I nodded, mumbling, "she's got jokes."

We shared a few smiles and finally, my smile sobered.

"Wait, your dad is letting you go to a party?"

"Yeah, I know, right? I think he's got a date or something that night. Who knows?"

I stared at her, wondering if she was serious.

"It'll be the one night he's not looking over my shoulder and I won't be able to spend it with my one true," she paused and then said, "high school classmate."

My grin turned into a full-on smile, stretching from ear to ear. I pulled her in close and we embraced again until the school bell rang, informing us that lunch was officially over.

Chapter Thirteen

The Past

After Science, Drake and I stepped out of the classroom. Before class, I had no clue what electro-negativity was and after class, I still had no clue what electro-negativity was.

"I definitely need a tutor," I said.

"Hey, is that Ashley," Drake said, pointing down the hall.

I glanced over toward the raised voices. Ash stood in front of Kurt with her finger stabbing him in the chest.

Drake and I took off without another word to see what was happening. We fought through the crowd of nosey kids holding their phones in the air, recording every moment of the encounter.

"Why don't you try me, little boy," Ash threatened. Her threats pierced into his slim frame as he set his gaunt eyes on her.

Another girl reached for Ash's arm, trying desperately to hold her back. But Ash's words hit their mark and the threats continued.

"I'd love to try it on you, little girl," Kurt said. His words were slow and menacing.

I stepped between Ash and her opponent.

"What's going on?" I asked, but my body quickly jerked back.

"Nah, I got this," Ash said. She turned her attention back to Kurt and raised her voice again.

"You touch her or any other girl and I will bust your head to the white meat. Do I make myself clear?"

The crowd erupted in ohs and ahs. The sound of more beeps from newly arrived phones burst between the laughter and applause of the crowd.

"That's enough! Break it up."

I turned to find three teachers barreling through the crowd, trying to disperse the hungry students. One teacher grabbed Ash by the hand and pulled her back.

"Come with me, young lady," the teacher commanded.

Ash didn't speak. Her eyes went to the teacher and then back to her red-faced opponent. Then she turned and walked away.

The girl who tried to hold Ash back initially was now jumping up and down, protesting to the teacher. Her pleas fell on deaf ears, but she continued anyways.

"It was him. She was helping me. You have to *get* him." The teacher brushed off the girl and continued escorting Ash to the front office.

□■□■

Later that night, Chance the Rapper blared through my earbuds as my eyes glided across the textbook. My head bobbed up and down, becoming too heavy as my tiredness slowly won the day's battle. My head gradually lowered, finding refuge in my textbook.

Suddenly, my desk trembled from the vibration of my phone, sending my head snapping back. Ash's emoji popped up, indicating a text message.

"Miss me?"

"Are you okay? What happened?"

"I'm okay. You good?"

"Yeah, but I didn't get dragged to the office. Why were you yelling at that dude?"

"That pig had his hands all over that girl. You should have seen her. She was so scared."

"And you stuck up for her?"

"Hell to the yeah."

"That's cool."

"What is?"

"You standing up for her. That's really cool."

"☺"

"Need me to handle him?"

"What are you going to do? Challenge him in basketball?"

"Uh…that was the plan."

"I don't need a man sticking up for me. I got this."

"Guess so. You know, that was pretty hot, actually."

"Whatever… Goodnight, Big Head!"

"Night!"

Chapter Fourteen

The Past

On Monday, the bell rang and the students raced out of the room. I threw my bag over my shoulder, excited to have escaped another one of Mr. Shelbey's lectures about the beauty of wildlife; today, the fantastic gray wolf.

I scanned across the hallway and saw Ash coming out of her class. Her black oversized hoody and sweatpants were a change of pace. It was a weird look for her. I mean, she looked good, but she looked good in everything. But I did prefer her usual tight jeans and a pro-black women's pride t-shirt.

"What's up, Ash," I hollered out. She looked up at me, but there was no smile, no eyes lighting up, nothing. She paused and stared. But as I approached, she turned and rushed away.

"*What the hell,*" I thought.

I caught up to her, placing my hand on her shoulder. She jumped back, accidentally slamming into the girl next to her.

"Hey," the girl screamed.

Ash didn't say anything. She just kept walking.

"Sorry," I said while trying to catch up to Ash. The girl mumbled a few words, but I didn't have time or the patience to respond.

"Yo, Ash," I screamed. I finally caught up to her, but I didn't dare touch her this time.

"Would you stop, please? What's going on?" I asked, standing in the middle of her path.

She looked down as if she was scared to look at me. She held her notebooks in her arms, crossed around her chest. Her blinks were extended and I could hear her breathe heavily.

"Are you okay?" I extended my hand to her, but she shrugged at the action.

"Ash," I said. This time, my voice was calm. There was more concern than I had expected.

"I can't...," she started in a whisper-like tone, squeezing her eyes shut.

"It's okay. Did I do something wrong?"

She shook her head. "I can't do this right now."

"Do what? What are you talking about?" I raised my hands in defense. "What did I do?"

Tears clung to the corners of her eyes but didn't fall.

"Ash," I repeated.

She looked down at the ground. That's when I noticed the shaking. It was subtle but definitely there.

"Are you okay?" I asked. My voice was more apologetic than anything.

"I'm sorry," she mumbled. Then she was gone.

I stood there, watching her disappear around the corner. I didn't understand what had just happened. I kept racking my brain, trying to remember if I had done something wrong.

"What did I do?" The answers never came. Instead, the only thing remaining was a tight sensation in my chest.

"Damn," I thought. I didn't know it at the time, but this was my first experience with a broken heart.

□■□■

Later that day, I looked down at my phone and clicked on the text messages. I scrolled until I saw Ash's avatar, Shuri from the Black Panther movies. No new messages. All I saw was a screen filled with countless unanswered text messages.

"Ash, are you okay?"

"What happened? Are you okay? Are we cool?"

"I don't know what I did, but I'm sorry. You know I'd never hurt you. Hit me back."

"Ash!"

"I love you. You know that, right."

"Alright, whatever."
"Ash! Ghosting me, really?"

I closed my phone and tried to focus on Ms. Ritter as she went over the next chapter in another William Shakespeare play. My concentration was gone and thoughts of Ash swam in my head. Although she sat a few rows away, she felt more distant than ever. I turned my head and watched her.

Her lips were pressed tightly against one another as her eyes zoned down at her desk. Her untied braids hung over her shoulder, resting on her chest. The sun shined through the window, reflecting against the contour of her face. She was beautiful.

Suddenly, she turned her head and her eyes met mine. At that moment, the rest of the world ceased to exist. It was just her and me. I hoped she would smile, wink or do anything to show she still cared. Instead, nothing. She turned back and her attention went back to her desk.

My memory of her faded, returning me to Mr. Haywood's class. An overwhelming sadness crept into my soul. I was sprung off a woman I would never have again.

I grabbed my things and headed out the door.

Chapter Fifteen

The Present

Knock Knock

"I got it," I said, making my way to the front door. I opened it to find Mr. Simmons standing with a plastic bag in his hand. His eyes were cold and he stared straight through me.

"Hey, Mr...." I began.

"Andre. You have to stop writing, my daughter," he said. His words crashed into my soul, taking me aback.

"Jackson, what's going on?" my mom asked.

Mr. Simmons' eyes bounced from me and then my mom and back to me. The thunderous thud of my heartbeat muffled every word he spoke.

"Andre here keeps writing Ashley letters and it needs to stop," he said.

I stared at him, not in fear but in comfort. He shared Ash's eyes. Those eyes had soothed me before, yet now they honed on me as if I was an enemy. Like, I wasn't wanted. Like my love wasn't wanted.

"I just thought...," I began.

"It. Needs. To. Stop," Mr. Simmons said. His baritone voice reverberated within me.

I stared at the translucent bag. My letters. All of my letters. I had hoped at least one would find her. At least one would find her and bring her back to me.

I looked up again as Mr. Simmons began walking away. He paused momentarily.

"She's not going to write you back."

The heaviness in my heart grew too much to bear and my soul collapsed within itself. My vision blurred with the stinging of my tears. All energy drained from within me and I stood as an empty vessel, not alive and not dead.

Before I knew it, the warm embrace of my mom's arms wrapped around me; my soul sank into the pain and I could feel every second I was away from Ash morph into some deep depression.

My mom held me like only mothers know how to and I cried. No, I sobbed into her arms.

My body trembled as I wished the pain would disappear. I wanted it all to disappear.

But my mind wouldn't let it. Instead, my thoughts went back to her and there was nothing I could do to stop it.

Chapter Sixteen

The Past

"Yo, there's your girl, Playboy," Rieko bumped my arm and motioned down the sidewalk.

Ash was pacing back and forth. Her hair was unkempt and her baggy clothes were covered in wrinkles. Her fingertips tapped their counterparts as her hands kept sliding in and out of her button-down sweater.

"Bro, she looks *messed up*. Is she talking to herself?" Rieko asked. I squinted to see clearer.

"Looks like it. Let me go see what's up," I said.

"Playboy, be careful. You know how these ladies can be *CRAZY!*" I dapped him up and nodded at the rest of the guys.

As I approached, I could hear her mumbling to herself.

"What the hell is wrong with you? Just do it, already," she whispered to herself.

"Do what?" I asked.

She jumped back, startled at my presence. She quickly closed her sweater, wrapping it around her body tightly.

"What?" Her voice was raised. Giant bags rested under her bloodshot eyes. I stared into them, even though she wouldn't look into mine. All I saw was emptiness.

"Ash?" I stepped closer. "Ash?"

"Dre, don't," she commanded. Her hands flung up, blocking my advance.

"Don't what?" I shrugged. I took a step back. "What's going on with you? You're acting crazy. You've been acting strange for weeks."

"I'm fine, Dre." Her tone caught me off guard. "Just..." She waved her hand in the air, then closed it into a shaky fist. "Just leave me alone."

Suddenly, her eyes grew wide and her movement stopped. I followed her field of vision, but at first, I couldn't see what or who captured her attention. But then, it became too clear.

Kurt and Erik stepped out of a beat-up truck, flashing their middle fingers to the driver, whom I assumed was their dad. I was too far away to hear what they were saying, but I could only imagine it wasn't respectful.

I turned back to Ash. She bit her bottom lip as her head lowered and her eyes narrowed. She slid her hand into her sweater and kept it there.

Her words became garbled, too low for me to understand. My stomach churned as a sinking sensation came over me. I crept closer, stopping inches away from her. She jolted backward, realizing I was still there.

"What the hell are you doing?" I didn't wait for an answer. I shoved my hand into her sweater and wrapped it around her wrist. She tried to struggle and that was when I felt it. She saw my reaction. Her eyes grew wide, matching mine.

"Let go, Dre," she commanded through gritted teeth.

"What the hell, Ash?" I looked around, ensuring no one was watching. Then, I gently pushed her around the brick wall.

"You brought a freaking…"

"Shut up," she whispered, ensuring no one heard me. "Get off of me, Dre." She squirmed around, trying to break my grip.

"Ash, stop!" My voice raised higher than I expected. My eyes were burning through hers. "Just stop!"

Her eyes finally met mine. The love she once had for me was gone. Instead, there was a woman whose eyes were filled with hate and anger. I clenched my jaw and continued staring. She didn't budge and neither did I.

Finally, I mouthed the words, "Stop, please." I wanted her to listen. I needed her to listen.

Her posture sank. A soft whimper emerged as tears began to slide down her cheeks.

"You can't do this. I won't let you do this, Ash. I won't." I shook my head and stepped closer so my body was inches away. I felt her heart race as my chest pressed against hers. Her warm breath flowed over my neck.

I scanned the area, ensuring no one was watching and quickly slid the gun out of her waistband into my backpack. As the weapon dropped inside, she erupted.

"He ruined me! Do you not understand?"

Ash knelt as her back pressed against the brick wall, crying into her hands. Her shoulders curled forward and she crumbled with every breath.

"I'm not *me* anymore. I've tried so hard." Her tears flooded the cement behind her.

"I tried so hard to go back to the way things were. I can't. I just can't."

She paused, forcing a steady breath.

"I don't want to be here anymore," she cried.

"It'll be okay; let me help you," I pleaded.

"You can't help me; no one can."

"Ash!" There was so much I wanted to say, but I was lost in an unfamiliar world. I feared that even if I gave her all of me, it still wouldn't have been enough.

I stared as she rocked, filling the silence with her tears. She let out an extended breath and stood.

Ash stepped closer, placing her hand on my chest. I stared at it, realizing this was the first time she had touched me in weeks.

"I'm sorry. I'm fine, Dre. I'm just tired. I need to sleep." Her voice found its calm; a unique peace flowed through her words. "I'm going to go sleep."

"Ash, I'll go with you. Let me go with you." I reached out for her hand, but she pulled away.

"No!" she barked. Frustration was painted on her face as she realized her tone. "No, I want to be alone. Please, let me be alone. You can't fix me." She placed her palm against my cheek. It was rough and dry, but it still felt like home. "I know you want to, but you just can't."

She leaned in and hugged me. I wrapped my arms around her and when my palms found her back, her body twitched, but she didn't pull away. I tried to hold her until the end of time.

She tilted her head and whispered, "I'm sorry. You deserve better." Then, she disengaged.

I nodded, not fully understanding the gravity of her pain or her words. She bit her lower lip and stared into my eyes. They weren't the same. Those eyes weren't my Ash's eyes.

As she began to walk away, I reached out for her hand.

"Then, promise me one thing," I said.

She turned her head, not entirely looking back.

"Promise we can talk tomorrow."

She paused and looked down.

"Promise!" I demanded.

Her response felt like it hung on the tip of her lips before finally floating to my ears.

"Promise," she said.

My hand slowly unwrapped around hers as I watched her walk away.

Chapter Seventeen

The Past

When Ash disappeared amongst the cars in the parking lot, I turned and was in motion before I could even think.

"Dre, you good?" I heard Rieko ask, but I didn't stop. My feet bounced against the pavement and my heart pounded in my chest. I pushed my way through the school entrance, bumping into fellow students until I saw him.

My arms extended until my palms pressed against his little brother's back. The force sent him flying through the air, landing painfully on the ground. Then I turned to Kurt, whose eyes went wild with shock.

While Kurt watched Erik plummet to the ground, my forearm pressed against his neck, slamming him into the locker. My body tensed as heat flushed within me.

The sound of ohs and ahs erupted nearby, adding to the hectic scene. Kurt stared down at me while struggling to create distance between us.

"What did you do to her, Kurt?" I screamed.

My forearm jerked forward as I pressed my weight against him. A slight gasp escaped his lips.

"Tell me!" I commanded.

Kurt's eyes flushed red. I could fill my adrenaline spike even more. His lips parted to speak, but before he could mutter a single word, my body was shoved off him.

"What the hell do you...?" Erik started. He must have gotten off the floor, searching for revenge. But I didn't allow that to last long.

My hand flew through the air, connecting securely against his chin. His knees buckled and his body collapsed to the floor.

I turned back to Kurt. He was slumped over, hands on his knees, as he tried to recover his breathing. When he noticed his brother his eyes widened.

Stepping forward, I huffed a breath and my fist flew through the air. Before I could smash his chin, my body felt resistance as something pulled me back. I turned, expecting Erik, but instead, Mr. Haywood stood.

"Andre! That is enough," Mr. Haywood yelled.

Rage and anger pulled inside of me.

"Let go of me," I roared, waving my arms, trying to get free.

I stared into Kurt's eyes and he stared back. He wiped a trickle of blood from his nose and smiled…that smile.

I closed my eyes and took a breath. For a brief moment I felt as if my soul had escaped my body. It floated above me and peered into Kurt's inner self. The demon inside him was just that, a demon fuelled by hate and anger. There was no light within him. No hope.

When I opened my eyes, a realization came over me. The realization that he had no remorse for what he did to Ash and he wouldn't stop. He would never stop unless I stopped him first.

I pushed Mr. Haywood away, escaping his firm grip and sprang to Kurt. My fists pounded his face. With each punch, I felt bones breaking. I wasn't sure if it was mine or his, but I didn't care at the time. All I saw was red. All I felt was hate. At the time, all I wanted to do was hurt him.

Multiple teachers and a security guard pulled me off of Kurt. As they dragged me away I stared into the crowd of students waving their cell phones.

A girl with blonde hair covered her mouth in disgust. A boy I recognized from the basketball courts threw his fist in the air as he shot me the biggest smile. My heart paused as a young girl with mesmerizing grey eyes stared at me. She shot me a slight smile and mouthed the words, "It'll be okay."

Chapter Eighteen

The Past

The school called my parents and my mom came to pick me up. My dad was at work but promised to meet us at home as soon as possible. I sat outside the principal's office, watching her and my mom converse.

I couldn't hear what they were saying, but occasionally my mom would nod, shoot a glare at me and then nod back at the principal again. Moments later, she walked out of the office, motioned for me out the door and hopped in the car without saying a word.

As she drove, my hands throbbed as blood spray painted my knuckles and fingers. I searched my bruised hands to determine whether the swelling indicated a break. I didn't think so, but the pain said otherwise.

When I looked up, I realized my mom had parked the car in a Jack-in-Box parking lot. Then she shut the car off and sat there, rubbing her temples as a slow, steady breath escaped her lips.

I lowered my head down, massaging my hands. Tiny goosebumps emerged on my arms, which I assumed were from nerves. Her voice emerged from the silence, barely above a whisper.

"Do you want to explain why there is a busted-up little boy in the nurse's office right now, Dre?"

"I…"

"Boy, we taught you to look at someone when speaking to them, so you'd better look at me," she commanded.

I turned to face her.

"I think," I paused. I swallowed. "I think he did something to Ash."

"Did *something*? Dre, what are you talking about? What did he do?"

I lowered my head, staring at the floorboards. The conversation with Ash replayed in my mind; all I wanted to do was run, run to her.

"Dre," she said firmly.

My eyes once again met hers.

"I think he…," I started. My stomach turned as I built up enough courage to continue. "Abused her. Like…" My words faded as I glanced out the window. The pain was too much and I simply stopped talking.

My eyes focused out the window, but I could hear my mom take a harsh breath and sigh.

"Oh," she said.

I wasn't sure what I had expected her to say. Heck, I didn't know what I was supposed to say. But either way, neither of us spoke a word. We allowed the silence to fuel the conversation.

Suddenly, the jingling of the keys burst through the silence as the car turned on. My mom let out another breath and finally spoke. Her words lost all harshness, all strength.

"Don't tell Miracle."

I squeezed my eyes, holding back my tears.

"Do you hear me?" she asked. "Do not tell your sister."

I sighed and nodded. With that, we drove home in silence.

Chapter Nineteen

The Past

When my mom and I came home, we walked into the apartment to find my dad already there, talking on his phone.

"Yeah, thanks for letting me know. He just walked in. I'll let you know if I find out anything," he said.

He stared at his phone for a second, exhaling deeply. My mom tossed her purse on the end table and moved to his side.

He turned and glanced at my mom. They studied each other for a moment, exchanging a conversation I couldn't understand.

"Dad, I'm sorry I…."

"Stop," he ordered. "Andre, have a seat."

I knew I was in trouble. He only called me Andre on two occasions and neither of them was good.

"Yes, Sir," I said.

I lowered my head and pulled out a chair at the table. He sat across from me and mom stood behind him.

I glanced back over at my mom and I could see the disappointment on her face. I didn't plan on beating up Kurt; it just happened. But I had to own up to it. That's what men do. At least, that's what my dad taught me to do.

"Dad, I apologize. This was totally…"

He held up his hand to silence me. I stared at him. But he avoided eye contact. I could see his eyes twitching back and forth as if he was solving a complex puzzle in his mind. Then, he looked up and spoke.

"It's Ashley," he said. "Her parents found her around an hour ago."

My heart imploded as the room spun around me. His words lingered in the air. I stared at his lips, but his voice became foreign. Words flashed in and out, but only a few made their way to the surface.

"On the floor…knife…note…."

I just sat there, frozen in time. I didn't understand. None of this made any sense. I was just talking to her.

My dad sat in front of me, staring into my eyes. I stared at him, but my mind was somewhere else. His lips moved again, but the words were muffled. His eyes narrowed as he leaned forward.

"Dre?" I finally heard him say. "Dre, do you understand what I said?"

I nodded.

"Dre?"

I nodded again. Then, somehow, I found myself on my feet, walking to my room. Each step was heavier than the last.

"Where are you going?" my dad asked.

I closed my bedroom door, leaving their muffled voices behind. I pressed my back against the door and squeezed my eyes shut.

"How could she be gone?" I asked myself.

The question repeated in my mind on an endless loop. I stood there for what seemed like hours. Every moment I had with her replayed like an infinite movie.

The thought of her sent me crumbling to the floor. Every inch of me shook. Tiny needles pricked the inside of my skin, piercing my flesh and everything within it.

I kicked at the air and my arms flailed at the openness. I punched existence in the chest, hoping to wake from this terrible nightmare. But nothing changed. Instead, I sat, brokenhearted and less of myself.

After a while, my hand inadvertently slid on top of my backpack and the heaviness of it brought me back to reality. I leaned over, peering inside it.

I stood and carried the bag to my closet. Lowering a stack of shoe boxes down from the top shelf, I grabbed the gun from my backpack and tucked it inside one of them.

"Ash," I whispered, shaking my head. "Was this for him or was this for…." The thought momentarily froze me.

I set the boxes back on the top shelf, ensuring the heavier container was positioned on the bottom of the stack. I reached into my pocket, trying to find a pen or something to mark it, making it easier to identify later.

A soft object caught my attention as my hand roamed my jean pocket. I pulled it out. My heart sank as I stared down at Ash's bracelet. She must have slid it into my pocket when she gave me that hug. That last hug.

Once again, my body crumbled to the floor as my heart grew heavy. It was as if I had forgotten how to breathe. I crawled into a ball as I clung the bracelet tightly to my chest. My tears flowed and my only thought was, *'How could Ash be gone?'*

Chapter Twenty

The Present

Later that night, I ran my finger along with the red bracelet. The material felt home to my fingers as my mind swirled with past thoughts.

"Baby, you want some more cobbler?"

I looked up to see my mom holding out the aluminum container of half-eaten peach cobbler.

"Nah, I'm good, mom," I said.

"Well, I'll take his piece," my dad said quickly, shoveling the leftovers onto his plate.

"You, okay?" Miracle whispered.

I hadn't really spoken to her since she returned from Kim's. I knew my mom wouldn't want me to tell Miracle about Ash's dad; honestly, I didn't know how to tell her.

I turned to her, "I'm good."

"Yeah, whatever. You never turn down cobbler," she said.

"You practically came out of the womb eating my peach cobbler," my mom said, placing the empty container in the middle of the table.

"Gross," Miracle snapped.

"Girl, hush up and eat your food," my mom said, throwing a potholder at her, which she successfully batted away. She shot my mom a smile.

"You okay, Dre?" This time it was my dad asking.

"Guys, I'm good. I was just thinking about…."

My mom held her head down; she knew. Miracle shot me a puzzled look and then stared at my dad, who just shrugged.

I had to convince them I was okay, for their sake. An idea sprinted to my mind and I went with it, hoping they would believe it.

"Dad, you should have seen yo boy on the court today. Breaking ankles all over the place," I said.

My arms swayed back and forth as if I was dribbling the ball.

"You know you get your skills from me, right?" My dad extended his arm as if he was shooting a ball. "Swish, baby."

"Uh, babes, you played on the freshman team," my mom said.

"And what's wrong with that," Miracle asked.

My mom placed her hands on her hips and tilted her head. "Nothing except he was a senior."

Miracle and mom shared a few laughs at dad's expense.

"There's no way the other teams would allow that," Miracle said.

"Sweety, after seeing him play, they encouraged it," my mom joked.

"Dad, is that true?" Miracle asked between chuckles.

"What? Y'all know your mom is lying," my dad said.

"So, where's your letterman jacket, then?" my mom asked.

My dad scooped some cobbler into his mouth. "See, what had happened was…." He scooped another mouthful in, purposely mumbling his response.

"Mmhmm, that's what I thought," my mom joked.

Miracle nudged me. "Guess you got your moves from mom."

I smiled. "Guess so."

After the laughter died down, I used that opportunity for my escape.

"Aight, I'm going to bed. See y'all tomorrow." With that, I said my goodnights and headed to my room.

I closed my bedroom door behind me and locked it. I proceeded to my bed and grabbed a piece of paper from my nightstand. I jotted a few things down, placed the paper back into the drawer and closed it.

Then I stood, peering down at the plastic bag of letters. My breaths were deep, deliberate and my mind was made up.

I walked to the closet and grabbed the fifth shoe box from the stack.

The weight was heavier than the others. Holding it in my hands, I paused and slid the top off. My hand slid inside and then I pulled it out.

The cold metal was heavier than I remembered. My finger roamed alongside it, feeling every nook and cranny, trying to give myself a crash course fast.

I held it up, teasing the trigger with my finger. Then, I stood up and pointed it at the dresser mirror; the movies made it seem so easy…another deep and deliberate breath.

I stared into my reflection's eyes. I was not born a killer. I didn't have it in me. But could I? There was only one person I was meant to kill. I swallowed hard and placed the gun to my temple.

Chapter Twenty-One

The Present

My heart raced as my chest heaved up and down. I could feel my hand trembling with every breath.

I let out a deep breath and slowly counted down.

"5….4…."

My heart ached as my pulse boomed in my ears. My grip tightened as the shaking became overwhelming.

"3…2…"

I slammed my eyes shut, breathed in and held it.

"1!"

Time slowed as my finger hugged the trigger.

Click, click

My eyes flung open as sweat trickled down the side of my head. I let out a shaky exhale as my nerves grew frantic.

"Oh my God."

The shaking was worse now. I tried to calm myself, closing my eyes and steadying my breath. *Breathe*, I reminded myself. *Breathe.* I looked down at the gun.

"Oh my God," I cursed. "The safety…"

I looked up at my reflection. A pained stare looked back. I didn't recognize the young man staring back at me.

Suddenly, a voice sprang from the other side of my bedroom door, causing me to jump and nearly drop the gun.

"Dre?" A gentle tapping came next. It was Miracle. I paused. I didn't know what to do. I didn't have time to put the gun back in the shoebox and hide it.

"Hey, Dre, can I come in?"

The doorknob rattled. Thankfully, the lock did its job.

"Yeah, one second," I said, sliding the gun into my backpack.

I wiped the sweat away from my forehead and opened the door.

Maybe she didn't expect me to answer because she stood there motionless in the doorway. But one thing was clear; her eyes were filled with sadness.

"You, okay?" Her voice was steady. Calm.

"I'm fine." I tried to smile. I'm sure it looked as awkward as it felt.

She didn't respond. She just stared at me for a moment. Even the best liars can't hide things from their families.

"I'm fine, Miracle. Promise."

She nodded her head and bit the corner of her lip.

"Mmhmm. Well, if you ever are not fine," she paused, "let me know."

I smiled. This time my smile was genuine.

"I will."

She turned to walk away. Then stopped.

"We still going to Kim's tomorrow?" she asked.

"Yes," I said. I had hoped she missed the slight hesitation in my voice.

"Promise?"

There it was. The same question I had asked Ash before she… How could a simple question tear my soul up and have a train of emotion come barreling down on my inner being?

She turned back and stared.

"Do you promise, Dre?" Her voice was stern as if she knew.

"I promise."

She sighed and looked down at the floor. There was more she wanted to say. Probably more promises she wanted me to provide or assurance that her brother would still be around tomorrow morning.

"Miracle." Her eyes met mine once again. "I promise."

She nodded and slowly walked away. I closed the door and pressed my head against it, shutting my eyes to focus on my breathing. I looked down at my hands as they trembled.

Chapter Twenty-Two

Love letter #365

Dear Ash,

It's been a year since you left me and I haven't really recovered. I may never recover. Tonight, the pain was too much for me. The pain and sadness I feel for you, it's like losing my eyesight. One day I can see the beauty of this world and the next it's nothing but darkness. Losing you is like that. You were my light.

Today, I did something stupid. Well, I almost did something stupid. I thought there was no way out of this hole. There was no end for me.

But it didn't end like it was supposed to.

I paused for a second.

Or maybe it did. After it was said and done, I realized I had things to live for: my mom, dad and Miracle. Hell, even Rieko.

This letter is not to make you feel bad. It's the opposite. This letter is for you to understand that my life can go on without you. I need it to go on without you because I don't have a choice. I love you and I know you love me too. I know it! I'm sorry for everything and we will be together one day. Just not today.

I love you and always will.
Dre

Chapter Twenty-Three

The Present

My feet pressed against the ground as sand crept between my toes. A soft breeze brushed against my cheek, sending a slight chill down my arm. The smell of the ocean refreshed my soul as I walked down the beach. The chirping of seagulls serenaded my journey.

The sunset looked like a love song. A smile appeared on my face as my eyes scanned the openness. I jolted backward as I saw a familiar face sitting on a bench. Ash turned to me and smiled. She patted the seat next to her, inviting me to join her.

I nodded and then approached. When I sat, there was a delightful silence between us. It was as if we were embracing each other's essence.

"It's beautiful out here," I said, staring at the horizon.

"It is." Her voice was soft.

A wave pounded against the beach, sprinkling reminisces of the ocean onto our faces. My hand shot up to block my face while Ash closed her eyes and allowed the sea to splash against her cheeks. A smile set on her face.

"I miss you," I said.

"I miss you too."

She placed her hands on mine and interlocked our fingers. Her boney fingers fit perfectly in mine.

I turned to see her face. Her silhouette was brushed with an orange, purplish angelic glow, the effects of the beautiful sunset. Her tongue was pressed against her top lip. My smile grew wider.

"I could have helped you. I could have…" I started.

She placed her finger against her lips, silencing me. She continued to stare off into the vast ocean. Time stood still as we watched Poseidon's masterpiece come alive.

The ocean always amazed me. It was filled with a world of life and beauty, yet it had the power to destroy just as much. At that moment, I chose only to see it for its beauty.

"You shouldn't be with me. Not yet," she said.

Her words hit deep, but I knew she was right.

"I know. I was about to…"

"I know," she interrupted. "But not tonight. Not right now. We'll be together soon enough. Do you understand?" Her fingers gripped tighter.

"Yeah."

"I need you to live for both of us, okay?" she asked.

"Okay," I said.

We sat there staring, hoping life could return to how it used to be. I knew this was a dream, but unlike the others, I wanted this one to last forever.

My eyes opened, revealing a new day; a new chance to carry out Ash's desire to live my life. I sat up and stretched out my arms. The sun beamed from the window, painting a heat stroke along my skin. I turned to the clock, which read 7:45. That was the first night I slept the entire night in over a year.

Chapter Twenty-Four

The Present

Throughout the morning my mind was clearer and a unique beauty rested in my soul. Last night was a mistake and it shouldn't have happened. I shouldn't have let all the pain and sadness win. I vowed never to let it happen again. I wanted to change. I had to. For Miracle. For my mom and dad. For Ash. Heck, for myself.

As promised, Miracle and I headed to Rieko's apartment. He had a few new beats for me to listen to and she would hang out with Kim and study for an upcoming test on Monday. I had secretly planned to give Rieko the gun. I figured he could get rid of it without asking too many questions. I couldn't have this get back to Ash. But first, as usual, we had to get our red Slurpee magic on.

As we entered the convenience store, the little bell at the top of the front door announced our arrival. I shot Kumar, a nod. He was rocking an old L.A. Lakers jersey.

"Dang, I didn't know they still sold Magic Johnson jerseys," I thought.

As I admired his throwback jersey, I accidentally slammed into the back of Miracle. She stood frozen in the middle of the store, staring down the candy aisle.

"What are you doing?" I asked.

She gestured down the aisle and that's when I saw them; Erik and his boy Jake. With a new focus on life, I brushed their presence off. It wasn't worth our time.

"Let's get out of here," Miracle commanded.

"Nah. We ain't letting no skin-heads stop us." I stepped passed my sister and preceded to the Slurpee station.

"Red, right?" I asked.

She hesitated but eventually nodded in agreement. I lowered the knob as the icy goodness began to seep out. My eyes stayed glued on Erik. Although my mindset had changed, I still didn't trust him.

"Hey," I whispered to Miracle and motioned to the nacho bar.

There was fear in her eyes, but I figured if I kept my cool, maybe she would too. She hesitated but eventually grabbed a black container filled with stale chips.

The two guys walked to the front of the store, carrying a few bags of candy. Erik's eyes met mine. The look was brief, but it was enough to put me back on my guard.

His chubby friend started giggling like a little schoolgirl as he tried to fling a licorice stick in his mouth. The tip of the licorice smacked the side of his mouth a few times as he tilted his head, trying to pop it in. Although slightly comical, I don't think his foolish attempts made him any less intimidating.

"A package of Ultras," Erik ordered. He threw a $20 bill on the counter and stared down Kumar until the order was finished.

I wanted Kumar to smack the hell out of him or throw his money down and yell, "your money is no good here," but that didn't happen. Kumar completed the transaction professionally, bagging the items and handing the little thug his change.

The two headed out the door, eventually climbing into their black jeep. Loud music blared out of the non-existent windows as they pulled out of the parking lot.

Whack!

"Ouch, what's that for?" I asked, turning my attention back to Miracle. Her arms were crossed and she smirked with one eyebrow raised.

"That's for acting tough, lil' boy. You're outnumbered, Dre!"

"Are you serious? It's even. Two of us," I motioned between the two of us, "and two of them."

"Me?" she questioned, sticking a finger to her chest. "Boy, I'm a lover, not a fighter."

"I'm sorry you're a what?" I said, crossing my arms. "Who you loving?"

"What? Oh, not like that." She waved me off as she finished prepping our snack.

"Mmhmm. I'm telling dad," I joked.

Whack!

Chapter Twenty-Five

The Present

As the dry air pressed against our lungs (the joys of living in the Mojave Desert) we cut through the dirt path behind a huge industrial building with multi-colored gas tanks stored along the side. This wasn't a shortcut, but it didn't have as much traffic as walking down Sierra Highway.

As we walked, I played a game of soccer with medium size rocks, sending them hurling a few feet away with my foot. Miracle entertained herself by admiring the sandy floor when a black jeep came speeding by, kicking up dust and dirt.

We turned our heads away, covering our eyes and coughed furiously. I turned back to the jeep, my eyes forced to squint due to the debris floating in the air. An object emerged through the dust clouds, flying towards us. I managed to jump back, but Miracle wasn't so lucky.

A huge thud emerged from my right as the object found Miracle's cheek. My jaw dropped, watching a mixture of melted cheese and beans slide down her face.

"Oh snap," I said.

"What the hell?" Miracle yelled, tensing her entire body.

The driver teased us, revving his engine rapidly. Without thinking, I knelt and grasped a medium-sized rock.

The jeep began to advance slowly, but with one swing of my arm I hurled the rock, aiming for the back window. It seemed like it took forever before it found its target.

My aim was off and I completely missed the back window, but the rock made its way to the passenger side mirror. Just as well.

Bright brake lights flashed and then the jeep reversed rapidly in our direction. The driver's side mirror reflected a pair of dark, sinister eyes filled with anger. There was hate in them. Pure hate.

I looked at Miracle and her eyes grew wide. I regretted the rock, but there was no turning back now. One thing was for sure. I had to protect her. No one was touching my baby sister.

The jeep was mere feet from us as we dove out of the way, hurling our bodies onto the desert sand. I gasped as I hit the dirt but didn't have time to complain. I quickly got up and ran to Miracle.

"You good?" I asked.

I pulled her up to her feet. She brushed herself off and we both just stared as Erik and Jake climbed out of the jeep.

My nerves were on edge, but I had to keep it together for Miracle. I had to.

"Oh, you're in for it now, boy." Jake pointed a metal bat in our direction. His usually pale face was red with anger.

Each step they took added to the growing fear inside me. *"Think, Dre,"* I thought to myself. *"Think!"*

My solution came as the two inched closer. It wasn't a solution that would end well. But it was the only solution that I had. Nothing else would ensure my sister's safety. Nothing.

I took one final look at my sister, swallowed and then turned to face the approaching enemies once again. I knew what I had to do.

Miracle reached for my arm, but I shrugged her off. She couldn't stop me. If I didn't end it now, it would never end. I dreaded what the monster would do if he ever got Miracle alone.

"Dre!" My sister's words floated into the air, not reaching their intended target. I lowered my head and narrowed my eyes toward Erik. He was my target.

I thought back to Rieko showing me that one court case and how the guy got off. I opened my mouth and began speaking to Miracle, but my mouth was dry from the dirt and the words came out as a jumbled mess.

"What?" she asked. Her voice cracked; the fear had taken over. "Dre, what did you say?"

I licked my lips and repeated my last line. "I fear for my life. I fear for my life and yours."

I had to make sure she understood me and heard me completely.

"Do you hear me? I fear for my life and yours," I repeated. My tone was sharp and exact.

Erik was close enough. Jake lifted his bat into the air. From this short distance, I could see Erik's fingers tighten around the crowbar. I briefly closed my eyes and took a deep breath until I built enough courage.

My hand reached behind my back and the cold metal kissed my palm. I extended my arm with the 9mm pistol; the safety was off this time.

Chapter Twenty-Six

The Present

Their faces lost all color as fear crept into their souls. My left hand wrapped around my right as my finger slid over the trigger. My eyes were aligned with the sight, which was aligned with my target. Everything else in this world ceased to exist.

I pulled back on the trigger; the sound was explosive. My eyes shut as my hands jerked up and my body jolted back. I had never shot a gun before and the power of such a small weapon was unexpected. The distinct smell of gunpowder lingered in the air.

My hands shook. I wasn't sure if it was the force of the gun or just my nerves, but either way I didn't like it.

I could feel my heart pounding against my chest, trying to escape the confines of my body. My breathing was erratic, quick unrhythmic little exhales.

I returned the gun to the aiming position, not knowing if my opponents would counterattack with their own weapons. The scene quickly faded into vision as I saw Jake's hand pressed against his chest.

"Oh my God," I thought.

He wobbled a few steps as he screamed out for God. I guess every man seeks God during his last few seconds of life. His eyes rolled in the back of his head as his body collapsed to the ground, his face colliding with the dirt.

He was never my intended target. I looked past his still body to Erik, who had disappeared into the jeep, already speeding off. Erik never looked back.

Suddenly I heard a soft murmur next to me. I couldn't quite make it out; my ears still rang from the sound of the blast. Then it appeared again, but again too muffled to make out.

Like someone hit a switch, the world became audible again and the soft muffles transformed into Miracle's screams.

"Dre," she screamed, "what did you do?"

I tried to move, but my body wouldn't let me. It was as if I was frozen in that spot for eternity. But her screams quickly interrupted my catatonic state.

"Dre," she repeated.

I lowered my arms and turned to her.

"Run!"

Chapter Twenty-Seven

The Present

"Run! Run!"

Before I knew it, we both took off full sprints. Our legs stretched out as our arms flailed, driving our momentum forward. The city zoomed past as if it was just a blip on a map. Our feet sped through the urban jungle as we raced to our safe haven.

My mind was blank. All I could think of was to run. Run! My heart skipped as its beats synchronized with my footsteps as they pounded against the pavement. I turned to my right and Miracle's body was pressed forward as her arms sliced through the air. Her form was perfect, while mine was amateurish. She was a better runner than I was, but I kept up with her for the first time. Ever.

As I pushed on, thoughts crept into existence.

"What did I just do? What did I just do? I just killed him."

We stretched down Kirkland Avenue and Kim's apartment came into view. We were almost there.

When we got to the front of her steps, I collapsed as Miracle's body fell over the metal railing. We both struggled to breathe. I huffed as my head hung between my knees.

"What were you…," she started between bouts of breathing. "What were you thinking? What did you do?"

I could hear the fear in her voice. But more importantly, I heard the disappointment. Nothing I could say could justify my actions. I had no words.

Finally, I responded. "I don't know what I did." I paused to catch my breath. "It wasn't supposed to go down like that. I wasn't…. I wasn't supposed to shoot him."

My eyes grew wide as the realization of my actions set in. My chest tightened as prickly needles stabbed the inside of my skin. We sat for a moment as our breathing filled the silence.

"Let's get inside quick."

I looked up and her arm was extended out to me. I placed my hand in hers and she pulled me up. I quickly latched on, wrapping my arms around her and embracing her like never before. I held her, hoping the hug would take away the pain, wishing it could rewind the last hour.

"I am so sorry," I said. "I'm so sorry." My body trembled.

"Shhh. It's okay." She rubbed my back, squeezing me tighter; typical of Miracle to be taking care of me. *I* was the big brother.

"I won't tell anybody," she whispered.

The thought of her bearing such a secret broke my heart. I didn't want her involved. I had to protect her.

"Let's get upstairs," she said, motioning up the steps. I nodded.

She went first and I followed close behind. Every step was heavier than the last. All the adrenaline was gone and now I was operating on one desire; to protect my sister. Get her inside and get her safe. I could take care of the rest on my own.

Chirp Chirp!

My eyes grew wide as a voice shouted from behind us.

"Stop right there, you two!"

Miracle turned around first and her reaction sent shivers down my back. I turned to find a police car pulling up along the curb. Two officers were sitting inside. I took a deep breath and slowly made my way down the steps.

The funny part is that I don't remember walking down the steps. It was as if my body was on autopilot. When I came down, my body was frozen. All I could hear was my heart beating, reverberating inside of me. I wrinkled my face as the noise grew louder and louder, almost unbearable.

Boom boom!

Boom boom!

I wanted to put my hands over my ears, but my body wouldn't move. I could hear Miracle's voice faintly in the background; something about Geometry and her school books.

Boom boom!

Boom boom!

The beating grew intense. I could feel my body crumbling with every beat. As the sound grew, suddenly, it stopped.

Her voice reappeared. "His name is Dre. Right, Dre?"

"Move lips. Speak," I thought. *"Speak!"* my soul screamed.

"Andre. My name…" I paused, "my name is Andre." I looked down at Miracle and then looked back at the officer. "Sir."

"Well Andre, what are you doing here? You studying biology too," one officer said.

He was a slim white guy, maybe in his late twenties or early thirties. He had a haircut I'd often see the ROTC guys wearing at school. His badge was wrapped around a black band with blue in the middle and his nametag read: Gladwell.

My eyes went back to his face. "Geometry, Sir. But I do study Biology as well, Sir."

The officer adjusted his sunglasses. As he did, a tattoo became visible. It was in old English-type lettering. I squinted to read it: Valhalla.

He glanced to my right, where another officer, Officer Wright, was staring back at me. I must have missed him in my haze while I came down the steps. His partner glanced back at him and nodded.

I turned back to Officer Gladwell and then my heart froze. The young girl with grey eyes stood on the opposite side of the street. She gave me a pained stare as if she knew something I didn't.

I could feel tiny goosebumps emerge on my arms as I stared across the street. Her lips began to move. She was trying to tell me something.

"Remember your promise!"

"Promise?" I thought, "what promise?" I racked my brain for what she meant, but nothing came to mind. How did I know her?

"Well, you kids be good. Get out of here," Officer Gladwell said, bringing me back to reality.

"Always, Sir," I said.

I quickly glanced at the grey-eyed girl and began going up the stairs. As my foot hovered over the first step, I paused. The promise!

Chapter Twenty-Eight

The Past

"Andre, can you wait in here while I speak with your mom and dad?"

The man handed me a box of building blocks, which I gladly accepted.

"Okay," I said.

"We'll be right in this room, okay, Dre?"

"Yes, daddy!" I said.

As they made their way into the other room, I sat on the colorful rug and dumped the blocks over the floor.

I had never been in this room before, but it was definitely made for kids. Bright-colored drawings of various animals hung on the walls while baskets of balls and dolls were spread across the room.

I looked down at the sprayed-out building blocks and smiled. I was going to build the biggest fortress the world had ever seen and no evil aliens were going to take over the world with me around. I stacked a few blocks on top of one another; the blue on the red and the green on the yellow.

"Where did the orange block go?" I asked myself, looking around my area.

"Looking for this?"

I looked up to see an older girl staring back at me. She was maybe 14 or 15 years old and had a soft voice. She sounded a little like Madea with her funny accent. Her arm reached out to me, holding the missing orange block.

"Thanks," I said, grabbing it and placing it securely on the green block.

"Your eyes are pretty. I've never seen grey eyes before," I said.

She smiled.

"Thank you," she said.

"Is your mommy and daddy making you see a sicatrish too?" I asked.

"A psychiatrist? No. I'm here to see you, actually."

"Me? Why me?" I asked.

"You don't know me, but we're actually family." She handed me another block.

"Really?" My eyes shot up. I thought most of our family lived in Arkansas.

"There ain't nothing wrong with my baby!" My mom's voice boomed from the other room.

"Babes, stay calm. That's not what the doctor is saying. He just wants to run some tests. That's what you meant, right, Doctor?"

"Hey," the girl whispered. "Ignore them. They're just having…," she paused, "grown-up time."

"Ohhh," I nodded. "Grown-up time is when mom and dad lock their bedroom door," I said.

She let out a muffled laugh.

"Not that grown-up time. They are talking doctor stuff. You keep playing with your toys. And we'll just keep talking, okay?"

"Okay," I said, stacking two blues on top of each other.

"So, like I was saying, we're family and you know what family does?" she asked.

"What?" I asked.

"They look out for each other."

"Oh, I already know that. My daddy says I have to look out for my baby sister. Look," I said, pointing to Miracle sleeping in her stroller. "That's my baby sister and I'm a big brother and I have to look after her because I'm a big boy, see?"

I stood up and put my hand over my head, "I'm this tall."

The girl smiled, nodding her head in amazement.

"Yep, you are a big boy. Well, since you're already a great big brother, I need you to do one little thing for me, okay?" she said.

"What?" I tilted my head and leaned into her.

"It's simple. I need you to let Miracle go first."

"Huh?" I scrunched up my face. "What does that mean? Like she gets to eat the candy first? That's not fair." I protested.

"No, you can eat the candy first. But maybe, you can hold the door open so she can walk in first."

"I can do that. Mommy makes me hold the door open for her," I said.

"Good. Or, maybe, if there's a set of stairs, you can let her go up first. You know, simple stuff like that." The girl leaned forward, focusing her eyes on me. "Can you do that for me?"

"Okay, that's simple," I said.

"Always let Miracle go up the stairs first!" Her tone was like when momma catches me stealing cookies from the cookie jar when I'm not supposed to. I never understood why we had a cookie jar if we couldn't eat the cookies. They're cookies!

"Do you understand what I said," she asked.

"I think so," I said, rubbing the back of my neck. I glanced down at my arm and massaged the little goosebumps roaming the skin. *"Goosebumps are silly,"* I thought.

My memory quickly faded and I was once again brought back to reality. I turned back to the grey-eyed girl, but she was gone. Officer Gladwell raised an eyebrow and began motioning forward.

The promise: I stepped back and allowed Miracle to go up first.

Chapter Twenty-Nine

The Present

My mind raced as I climbed the steps. I decided to confess everything to the police by the third step. On the seventh step, I told myself to put Miracle inside so she would be safe. I had to convince them she had nothing to do with this. By the eleventh step...

"Gun!"

"Gun!"

My heart sank as the word echoed in my head. My shirt must have flapped open as I climbed the steps. I had forgotten it was there. My head spun around as my heart sank.

Officer Gladwell and his partner stood there, arms extended, hands squeezing their guns. They were aimed right at me.

My arms flung to the sky. I spread my fingers apart. Screams sprouted from their mouths.

"Put the gun down!"

"Get on the floor!"

"Do it now!"

"It's not like that, I swear," I yelled, at least; I thought I yelled. My inner being felt paralyzed and everything felt like a dream. I twisted my head side to side while my voice crackled, "I'll do it. I'll do it."

My entire body shook as I squeezed my eyes shut.

"Get down the steps now, son," Officer Gladwell shouted.

My eyes opened to see both him and his partner; their bodies were rotated slightly. Their eyes were aligned with their guns.

"Do it now, son!"

"Please." A whimpering voice came from behind me. It was Miracle. Her hands were stretched out as tears poured down her face. Her whimpers continued but fell on deaf ears.

"Okay, Sir. I'm doing it."

My eyes flipped from one officer to the other. I swallowed as I slowly lowered my right hand.

"I'm listening, Sir," I said.

I slid my hand behind my back, wrapping my fingers around the metallic weapon. I blew out an extended breath and stared at the officer.

"I'm doing it slowly, okay? I'm doing it," I said, trying to remove the panic in my voice. My hand slowly appeared from behind me. I could see the two grip their weapons even tighter.

"Get down from the steps!"

"Lower the gun," Officer Wright shouted.

My hand kept the gun high and I was no threat to the officers. I was never a threat to the officers, but in their world, you were either a friend or you weren't. Maybe this simple yet complex thought was the reason for so many deaths on both sides. I briefly closed my eyes and took in a deep, concentrated breath.

As my body rattled with fear, I stepped down and then again. I followed that pattern for a few more steps, keeping my hands high in the sky.

When I looked into Officer Wright's eyes, I saw a glint of fear. He was just as scared as I was, but he hid his fear well. I'm sure he had more experience in this situation.

"Slowly, son," Officer Wright said. A bit of sweat trickled down his brow. He bit his lip and there was a tightness around his eyes.

His partner seemed calm as if he had been through this before. I prayed his last time ended with everyone going home.

"That's it, keep coming, boy," the officer shouted.

I obliged, taking every step slowly. My stomach churned as I reached the fifth step. But, on the fourth step, my left foot slipped and my foot slid down two steps.

My body reacted instinctively, reaching my hands in front of me to catch my fall. My left hand gripped the metal railing as my right hand hit the top of the railing, unable to get a grasp because the gun was still in my hand. The gun was still in my hand.

Time slowed as my heart quickened. I inhaled a breath and kept it in. Moments later, I went deaf to the world as massive blasts threw my body against the apartment wall.

"Nooooo!" Miracle shouted.

Bump Bump

Another searing shot blasted through my flesh as my heart fought for survival.

Bump…Bump

My breathing slowed.

Bump……Bump

I opened my mouth and mumbled one final word.

Bump……..

"Ashley!"

……

Chapter Thirty

Over A Year Later

My dad cleared his throat.

"You sure about this?" he asked. His eyes were filled with sadness as his eyes scanned the room.

"Yeah, dad," Miracle said.

My dad stared at his precious little daughter. He nodded slightly, grinning at the amazing woman she had become.

"Okay, Bubble Gum." He chewed on his bottom lip for a second and then slowly walked away.

Miracle stood at the doorway to my bedroom, watching our dad disappear around the corner. Then, she stepped into the room, closing the door behind her.

She peered around the room, letting the past ghosts of our childhood roam free for one brief moment before setting the empty boxes on the bed.

She had volunteered to be the one to collect my things. The rest of the apartment was almost all packed and this was the last room anyone wanted to touch. The memories were too painful. Maybe that is why they were moving; a fresh start, a new beginning.

She scanned the walls, from the Kobe Bryant poster to a collection of pictures thumb-tacked to the wall. Her eyes widened as she reached for a picture in the middle of the wall.

The picture depicted younger versions of me and her arm-in-arm at Disney Land. Goofy was putting bunny ears behind my back and she smiled from guilty knowledge.

She ran her finger to another picture. A young man wore a dark blue suit with several rows of medals and military insignia pinned to its exterior. His lips were pressed against a young woman wearing a gorgeous white mermaid wedding dress.

"Aw, mom, you looked so beautiful," Miracle said, examining our parents on their wedding day.

She turned to my nightstand. Her attention quickly went to a picture sitting on top. She had found it months prior when she first came into my room. But then, it was faced down underneath a pile of papers. Now, it stood tall for the world to see. Thanks to her.

She lifted the image, smiling at its display: My arms wrapped around Ashley as she pressed into me. Our smiles were magic and the love we shared crescendoed off the canvas. I wished I could return to that day to have one last moment with her, to share one last laugh.

Miracle sucked in a breath and then gently placed the picture frame down as if it was a fragile relic that could disintegrate with the slightest breeze. With a little tug of the knob, the nightstand drawer pulled open, revealing a mess beyond words. Notebooks, papers and even candy wrappers filled the tiny compartment. I had always meant to clean it up; I just never got around to it.

She put a few items into one of the boxes. Some things looked like trash, so she tossed them in the grey bin alongside the nightstand. As she rummaged through the drawer, she picked up a handwritten note and began to read. Her heart instantly dropped.

Chapter Thirty-One

Over A Year Later

Dear family,

If you're reading this, I am no longer with you. I'm sorry for the pain this may and probably did cause. I'm sorry for the emptiness you may feel from this. I don't want you to be sad. I don't want you to blame yourself.

If you wondered why I did this, it's because I had to. Losing Ash was too much for me. It's hard to explain. She provided the air to breathe and I couldn't survive without her.

When she left, a massive part of me went with her. My heart wasn't the same. My soul wasn't the same. *I* wasn't the same. This was the only way I could be whole again.

Please know that I am finally happy. So, smile because Ash will take care of me, just like I know you'll care for each other.

Mom and dad,

You did everything right by me. You raised me right and I'm thankful Miracle has you as parents. THIS IS NOT YOUR FAULT.

Miracle,

You are an amazing little sister and I can't wait to see what amazing things you will do in the future. You're my best friend and I love you! Take care of mom and dad. They'll need you more than ever.

THIS IS NOT YOUR FAULT.

I love you all very much,
Andre King Jenkins

THE END

Suicide Hotline

We all go through dark moments in our lives. But you do not have to go through these dark times alone. Resources are available and people are willing to talk or, more importantly, listen to you. Don't give up. Your life is too valuable to lose.

National Suicide Prevention Lifeline
1-800-273-8255
Lifeline (suicidepreventionlifeline.org)

WAIT!

Thank you for spending your time reading my book. Your support means a lot and I do not take it for granted. If you have enjoyed this book, please leave an honest review where ever you purchased it. Every review helps me improve my writing.

Signed,
Your faithful author,
Rodney LaMarr

For more information on my upcoming projects, please visit my website at: **www.rodneylamarr.com.**